BRATVA PRINCE

BRATVA ROYALTY
BOOK 2

CARINA BLAKE

THE STEELE PRESS

ISBN: 9798375530109
Copyrighted © 2022
Carina Blake
All Rights Reserved

No part of this book may be reproduced, copied or transmitted in any form or by any means, electronic or mechanical, including photocopying, recording, or by any information storage or retrieval system without written expressed permission from the author, except in the case of brief quotations embodied in critical articles or reviews.

This is a work of fiction. Names, characters, businesses, places, events, and incidents are products of the author's imagination and are used fictitiously. Any resemblance to actual persons, living or dead, events or locales is purely coincidental.

Cover design: Bookin' It Designs

The use of actors, artists, movies, TV shows, and song titles/lyrics throughout this book are done so for storytelling purposes and should in no way be seen as advertisement. Trademark names are used in an editorial fashion with no intention of infringement of the respective owner's trademark.

This book is licensed for your personal enjoyment. This book may not be re-sold or given away to other people. If you would like to share this book with another person, please purchase an additional copy for each recipient. If you are reading this book and did not purchase it, or if it was not purchased for your use only, then you should return it to the seller and please purchase your own copy.

He took my family, so I'll take his.

Betrayed. My father had created ties with the Volcheks, and they repaid that faith with deceit, murdering my parents and my younger siblings. If they only had gotten to me, the empire they desired would have fallen into their laps. Unfortunately for them, my father's good deed will not go unpunished. I will destroy everything they hold dear, end their bloodline.

That is until I see his precious hidden princess. She'll need a dark prince, whether she knows it or not. No will not be an acceptable option for the icy beauty.

PROLOGUE

ROMAN

THE STENCH of blood in the air still lingers, even though the bodies had been removed days ago. Their bodies are being prepared to lie in the cold ground in just a short while. A stiff breeze shoots through the room as if a window is open, although they aren't.

I stare at what remains of my family: just the darkened stains of their last moments down to the small pool of dried blood where my little brother bled out.

Standing in my brother's room and looking at his toys covered in his blood, rage and pain filled me up and hurt my soul. Of all the people to harm, a child should never pay the price. Violence had never been my strong suit.

My father had been disappointed that I was more of a financier than a hardcore killer because there were always more enemies looking to take over the Semyonov Bratva.

Smirking up at the ceiling, I think about all that is to come.

Well, Father, it seems I do have it in me.

"Boss, Roman." Alek's voice breaks through my mourning. My eyes slam shut as I try to control the burning anger in my chest and the annoyance at just the sound of his voice at the moment. "Alek, leave me be, or you will join these remnants."

"Sorry." He steps back and allows me to absorb the violent scene before me. This home used to be filled with so much love and joy, and now there's nothing left but misery and death.

It's the first time I've been here since it happened. If I'd been here, this massacre wouldn't have taken place. The coward wouldn't have struck with me around because he knew that my men and I were deadly even though we were quiet about it.

I wasn't a butcher, but I had men who could slice you up like the nicest, thinnest piece of meat. I loved to use a blade over a gun. It always felt more personal. My life hadn't been focused on the dark side, though. I tried to make money and grow financially rather than decimate my enemies. It was a fatal mistake that won't be made again.

Revenge, destruction, and absolution will be mine. As soon as I find out who did this, there will be hell to pay, and I will take no prisoners — show no mercy.

One of my father's enemies did the unthinkable, the cruelest action, but he left one of us alive. A mistake a killer can't make around other monsters. Did he think I was too weak to respond?

Well, he was wrong.

We had several other Bratvas across Russia and around the world who would love to take over all our territories and businesses, so the list of enemies could be endless, but something about this felt too close to home for it to be a stranger.

Although regrettable and worthy of revenge, my father's death is understandable because it was the business we were in. It was something he had signed up for when he'd taken over for his father and his father before him.

However, the senseless butchery of my mother and brother will not be tolerated with just his murderer's death. The annihilation of his entire lineage is a must. Nothing less will be acceptable.

"Forgive me, Roman, but it is time."

I look at Alek and although I want to snap his neck for the interruption, I know that my long-time friend is correct. "I am not ready to let them go," I confess.

He steps up and pulls me in for a brief hug. It's not something I would allow from anyone else besides my family. We step back. "No one is, but they will always be with you, and your revenge will ensure that their memory lives on."

"Can I trust that you'll be at my side?" The look in his eyes leaves me no doubt that he's one hundred percent with me. His eyes drop to the stained stuffed animals, and I know which one catches his eye. It's the one he gave my brother for his birthday.

He swallows hard and then says, "Until my dying breath, Roman."

I nod and then storm out of the room before I go crazy. My head needs to be clear for what's about to come. It will be one of the hardest days of my life and everyone will understand my grief; still, I have a mission to accomplish.

Today I'm allowed a hint of weakness, but only just a hint, so I square my shoulders and slide into the back of my well secured armored vehicle. We leave my former childhood home and head to the cemetery where my family is being laid to rest.

The drive to the cemetery is filled with silence as I consider those who would dare to attack my family and those who could have gotten that close. I'm certain tensions will be high as those in attendance will be looking for the culprit or worrying if my suspicions are on them.

Things might get ugly although our enemies didn't operate the old way anymore. Most attacks were done through your financials and killings were only handled by the street soldiers who didn't mind getting their hands dirty for a bonus. I hadn't killed anyone in years. Until this betrayal, I had planned on keeping it that way.

As I arrive at the entrance of the church courtyard and it's empty. My men park and scope it out before I exit. I walk up the steps of the church and, I'm met by the priest. "Mr. Semyonov, I'm sorry for your loss."

I shake his hand and look over to where the caskets have been set up in the middle of the altar in the distance. Taking a deep breath, I finally answer him. "Thank you, Father."

I've known Father Leo since I was a little boy and my father started bringing us to this church. Given what we did for a living, I never felt righteous coming to services. Still, I fulfilled my obligation as the bratva prince on my parents' behalf.

I haven't been here since I moved away and purchased my own estate about twenty miles from here. Now, I'm here for another reason. A terrible burden that I'm not ready to face. I'd never be ready for, but I have no choice but to handle.

"You will get through this one day at a time, my son."

His platitudes didn't soothe me, but I knew it went with the role he filled.

Still, I have pressing matters on my mind. "I must ask you. Was my father's effects taken off his body before he was taken into the funeral home?"

I examine his response, but I can't gauge whether he truly doesn't know, or he's lying. "Not that I'm aware of."

"His watch is missing." A stabbing pain rips through my entire body at the idea that someone dare take it from him.

"I can contact the men that brought him to the church and inquire."

This is a private issue that I'll be dealing with on my own. If his effects weren't taken, which I know they weren't, because his wedding ring was still on, that means his killer took it. "No, thank you. I will handle the matter."

"Please, no more violence." My temper boils instantly and I want to grab him by his collar, but I don't.

I tilt my neck, cracking it and taking a cool, calming breath before I address a man of faith. "Just worry about saying the prayers, father. My soul isn't asking for saving."

We move to the front pews while my men stay at the entrance of the church. Our seats are just feet from my family as we go over what will happen in the next hour. I can't stop glancing their way, hoping this is just a nightmare, even though I know it's not.

It's not long before the church bells begin to go off.

"Mourners will arrive shortly." And so will a traitor.

My family will not have the honored ceremony they deserve because their bodies do not need to be seen in such disgrace. All prayers and blessings will be at the burial. I will not host a gathering for mourners, as I will not break bread with my enemy.

"Are you sure you wouldn't like a small reception, Mr. Semyonov?" the priest asked as I stood next to the caskets of my beloved family.

"Someone butchered my family, and I refuse to pretend that this a good death or to share stories of my little brother with anyone," I bite out with more anger than I should give the man, doing his duty to my family and to God.

"Yes, forgive me. I understand your wishes, Mr. Semyonov." About damn time. I hate to repeat myself and this isn't something that was up for discussion. My family will be remembered when the time is right. For now, it would have to wait. I had a murderer to find.

"Leave me," I order all of them in a calm voice. The priest and my men step from the church altar, leaving me alone. Dropping to my knees, I send up a benediction that they find peace and their souls aren't searching the earth for long. I stand and place a kiss on top of each of their caskets.

The warmth that had made me strong for my entire life has frozen over and will now destroy anyone that dares challenge me, as the Russian winter has done to many. Even though I've turned to ice, I feel more dangerous than ever.

My men accompany the church members to bring my family to their final resting place. I'm the last in my line and it shouldn't have been that way. Holding back all emotion, I steady myself and follow behind the final casket of my little brother.

Slowly, the mourners gather around the dedicated burial, where the snow falls all around. My mother loved the freshly fallen snow, and my brother loved to practice tossing snowballs at my father and his men as he learned to aim, which made them all proud. He was everything sweet and strong, mixed all in one. I will miss them so damn much.

There were more lives lost that day, but none of them mattered much to me. My father had lost ten men in the raid on the home, but their services were held while I was gone.

I did send care packages to those who had families and thanked them for putting up a fight. It probably didn't mean much to them when they lost someone they loved, but it was my duty.

The priest begins his long eulogy of my family, starting with my beloved mother, who had the heart of an angel. I hold back all my emotions, from the tears to the rage.

As Russians, we don't show emotion except for the women and small children that have come. My mother's best friend clings to her child, and I look at her, knowing that she's breaking inside for more than just my mother's loss, but a mother's loss in general.

Alek and Ivan stand close to me, looking every so often at those in the crowd. There are at least a hundred mourners here. All of them are close to the family in one way or another. Ivan's mother and sisters have come to give their support.

I see my father's long-time friend Vladimir Volchek standing alongside his son, who is about my age of thirty. We used to be friends as kids, but we were raised with different values and I wanted nothing to do with him by the time we were fifteen.

The eldest Vlad doesn't meet my gaze, which surprises me only because of all people he shouldn't feel intimidated. Volchek's empire is larger than my father's, now mine. The way the muscle in his jaw ticks raises the hair on the back of my neck.

Still, I move my attention to the rest of those here to pay their respects. There are several other families present, but it's one face that I'm grateful to see even if I won't show it.

My childhood friend Drago Romanov came all the way from the U.S. to be here. He's a hulking beast of a man who says very little unless necessary. Right now, his body says more than his words could. His eyes continue to roam around the attendees for the same reason I am. He knows that it is those who are the closest to us that could be a danger to us.

Of all my guests, Drago is the last person I'd expect because he has no interest in living in Russia again. A visit for business or pleasure is rare because the icy cold streets had ruined his love for his homeland. He hardly even speaks Russian intentionally. The United States is home now and he doesn't have any intent on changing that. Even if he did, I couldn't imagine him coming to Russia. Maybe he'd move somewhere in Europe.

I watch as his gaze drops on Volchek, lingering on his son as well. He looks longer than is polite, and I hope to hell that he isn't right. Although he's familiar with Volchek, even in a minor business deal with him, he never cared for the man, which is wise. Could he know something I don't or is it just Drago's personality coming to the forefront?

A sinking feeling sets in my gut as the service comes to an end. My parents' killer is here, and I'm very well acquainted with them.

Everyone passes around the coffins as the flowers and sticks are placed on my family to protect them in the afterlife. Their *bad* death means they need help to go over to the other side, and I'll make that happen when I get my revenge. I'm the last to drop them onto the caskets, and the finality of it hardens my heart.

"I will avenge you," I whisper.

Once the service is over, Drago walks over toward me, sending the crowds parting like the Red Sea. We embrace as brothers, and he whispers in my ear, "If you need anything. I'll be a call away, my brother."

We separate and I nod. "I just might." I will need his assistance in due time when I have more to add to the matter, but this isn't the time or the place for such a discussion, given my heightened rage and suspicion.

As I'm about to address his visit, Volchek comes up to us. "Roman, my boy. I'm sorry about your loss," Vlad says, interrupting our conversation intentionally.

He doesn't wait for me to say anything before addressing Drago. Staring at him with an appraising look. "We've met before, haven't we?" Does he dare ask Drago that? Why?

"Yes, we were talking about my property in Omsk." He's going to pretend he doesn't know Drago in front of me, which makes no damn sense unless he's gauging our responses. They're both working with Anatoly Petrov on his massive buildings in Omsk.

"I'm always interested in expanding my empire." The liar. He'd rather keep everything small and isolated in his warm mansion. The only reason he's helping Petrov is that his family helped him like my family had when Drago was a young orphan. If Drago could stay out of Russia he would.

"Yes, we must get together to discuss it sometime," Volchek says, clapping my friend's shoulder. Drago remains cool, but I sense the icy threads that will get Volchek's hand chopped off if he's not careful.

"I return to America tomorrow." I don't like the quickly masked frown on Vlad's face. It reads of bullshit like he wants to meet with Drago about something much sooner.

"Perhaps you can have that discussion somewhere else besides my family's graves," I say through clenched teeth, getting rankled by his blatant disrespect to my family.

Volchek's face, for a brief second, showed its true irritation before daring to feign remorse, and that's all I needed to know. Am I staring at my family's assassin, or at least the man who orchestrated it? "I'm sorry, my boy. It's in poor taste."

"My apologies, Roman." Drago wisely creates a buffer between Vlad and me and then hands him a business card. "I must return to my hotel." I watch as my friend departs.

"You don't care for him much, Roman," Vlad says. I'm not a fool, no matter what he takes me for, so I play along.

"What do you mean?" I ask, pretending to misunderstand his meaning.

"Tension eased as soon as he left."

"I can't rule him out from being the one to kill my family. There's just something cold about that man." It's a lie that I tell with the straightest face. Drago may be cold, but he's not evil.

"It is strange that he quickly came from Chicago on such short notice." That's what a great friend does, especially because we live in a world of airplanes, but I don't say that. Strange, for a man who claimed he hadn't been acquainted with Drago, he'd known where he lived without even looking at Drago's business card.

"It is interesting. Excuse me, Volchek. I must say goodbye to my family, privately."

"I understand." He clasps me on the shoulders and then walks away from the graves without even paying his own respects. After knowing my parents for nearly twenty-five years, his behavior makes me more and more suspicious.

It's then that I see his son wrap his hand on his father's shoulder, giving me my damn answer to everything. It takes everything in me not to reach for my gun, blowing his head right off in front of the trailing crowd of people.

Alek and the rest of my men follow as the crowd exits the cemetery.

"So, you don't take Romanov as the one, do you?" Alek looks at me sideways.

"No, I was testing the waters." My eyes haven't left the spot where Vlad and his son had been standing when their exchange took place. Volchek hadn't hidden his disdain for me, even in my deepest hour of grief. No, he and his son stood by my family in their graves as they assessed my moves.

The younger Vlad had my father's watch on his wrist. It hadn't gone unnoticed, although I guarantee that was his intention. I wouldn't disrespect my family there, but my mind had never worked quicker as I considered all the ways to dispatch of the two along with every soldier that assisted in the crimes against us.

IT'S LATE IN THE EVENING, AND I'M SITTING WITH A GLASS OF my family branded vodka, thinking about today's services and my dogs at my feet. "Boys, we're going to get you some fresh meat to feast on," I tell my cane corsos, rubbing their heads.

Taking another sip of my drink, I recall my father's nearly ancient conversation with Vlad when I was twelve. "A hidden daughter."

A smile spreads across my face as I sit in my secured estate, thinking how to go about getting the information I need. It's time to call on my friend for his skills. "My brother. I need your help," I say to Drago.

"Whatever you need." Our lines are secure and untappable thanks to his technology.

"I need you to find someone, but it must be the most secret search possible." Drago is an expert at these things, and with Volchek probably keeping tabs on me, everything must be done through others — for now.

Without hesitation, he says, "I'm in." We end the call and I finally head to bed.

By the next morning, Drago sent me an encrypted file. Now, I had everything I needed to start my plan.

Here it is. There is the map of the vicinity and all the entrances.

Thank you, my friend.

Any time. Going home.

Evidence in hand, I consider my next moves. My retribution will not be easy or fast. It will be slow and methodical as I undo all that Volchek holds dear. Starting with his family.

CHAPTER ONE

ROMAN

TEN DAYS LATER

Alek enters my office with my breakfast, which has consisted of just coffee over the past week and a half. He sets it down in front of me before taking a seat in the chair in front of my desk. "Roman, everything is set up for the first round this morning."

"That's good news." I sip the hot black coffee with a sinister grin on my face as the plans I've been stewing over for more than a week fall into place. Sleep has been almost nonexistent for me since I learned who orchestrated their murders. Dreams turned into nightmares and I woke up with new ways to seek revenge on their killer.

The first domino will fall in an hour, and I will enjoy it as the world crumbles around Vladimir Volchek. I'll be saving his death for last, but not until I end everyone in his lineage and take every ounce of his empire from his old, cruel hands.

One by one, his companies, warehouses, and lives will fall.

To the world, Vladimir only had one child, his heir, Vladimir the second, a dreg of humanity, but he had a secret only a few had known about, a hidden daughter. Why she was a secret made no sense to me, other than to keep her away from his enemies like me.

Drago had come in handy, getting everything I needed to find the missing princess. It would only be a matter of time until she was next on my list. He could hide her all he wanted, but he unleashed a monster, and there was no way I could be tamed.

While we wait to strike, Alek and I go over my family's assets, which are massive on top of my own that I had accumulated outside of the Bratva. Financially, I was a guru of sorts, having gone off to college and getting a master's in business in both domestic and foreign for the purpose of legitimacy.

With both empires, I'm now a target for Volchek and maybe the reason he waited to come after me. What a foolish move on his part. He won't have a ruble to his name before I end his life. I want him broke with nothing to his name before I wipe him from the earth.

We don't have to wait the full hour when the call comes in twenty minutes later, and everything is ready to strike.

"Showtime." I rub my hands together before standing and adjusting my nicely tailored suit. It happened to be one of my mother's favorites and she often told me how handsome I looked in it. Today, I wear it in her honor as I take down the first of several targets. Time to make both parents proud.

Grinning, I ask my righthand man, "Ready, Alek?"

"Always. Let's do this." He pops up from his seat, and we both file out of my office over to the arsenal of weapons I have at my disposal. Although I have the special piece I want for today, I take a few extra just in case.

We prepare our weapons and head to my state-of-the-art, highly secured armored SUV. Our team had been there two hours earlier, setting up everything we needed for this to work like a well-oiled machine.

Given they had made themselves a target, it surprised me that they hadn't tightened up their security. Taking it as an insult, I doubled down on my will to destroy every enemy I came across. I'd crush every soldier of his who put up a fight.

Alek and I drive to the destination on the wharf, parking just out of sight.

There are no cameras in this area of the wharf. Still, I sent men ahead to do a cursory sweep of the rest of the dock before we arrived. Not that I'm worried about Volchek finding out it was me, but the less the authorities have on me, the less they can use against me.

As we moved closer we were approached one large man in a suit with a .357 in his waistband. "You aren't supposed to be here, are you?"

"Is that anyway to speak to me?" I challenged.

"You are the weakling son of a dead man. I've eaten meat tougher than you," he says, smirking boldly.

"Da?" I ask, smiling as well. Swiftly, my blade enters his carotid while another enters his gut. I pull them out and move on walking toward my targe. Quickly we dropped two guys without making any noise. They didn't even get a chance to radio in that we were there. Anyone stepping in my way will meet their maker today.

We stalked down to where Vlad the Second, my former playmate, was getting his rocks off by beating on a woman. She probably didn't serve him his morning drink properly. For a tough guy, he had the most specific way of having his coffee. It was so diluted with creams and sweeteners that it wasn't coffee anymore, *the little bitch.*

We're just out of sight, our bodies are hidden behind his SUV.

"Can't pick on someone your own size, Volchek?" I ask, stepping out from behind his vehicle.

His head shoots up, eyes wide and glassy, clearly on something. "What the fuck are you doing here?" he gasps, taking a step back from the broad on the ground.

She scurries back on her palms, looking to get away from danger. It's what happens when you work for a cruel, sick fuck.

"Is that any way to greet a long-time friend?" I ask, my tone belying my words. I open my arms and shake my head.

"Friend? I'm supposed to believe that we're still friends."

"I don't know what would make us enemies, Vladdy boy. Do you?" I ask, daring him to deny the truth or be bold enough to own his betrayal. Either way, he already had his fate sealed the second I learned he had a hand in their deaths.

The smirk on his face spreads into a grin. "You are weaker than my father thought. What are you here for? My men line this wharf. There's no way you'll get out of here safely."

It's my turn to smirk because they line the wharf alright. Bodies litter the area like trash, and I have one more to dispose of before all is said and done here.

"Oh, don't worry about my safety, Vladdy boy. We have matters to discuss, like why you were wearing my father's watch to his funeral. The one he never took off." He smiles, lifting up his cuff for me to see it on his wrist.

"He didn't need it anymore." I nod my head several times with insane patience, which gives Vlad a chance to reach for his weapon, but he's not as fast as me.

"You don't either." I fire one shot into his head, and he drops to the ground before he gets a shot off.

I turn my attention to the woman on the ground. She didn't scream when I blew a hole through his head, a side-effect of years in this life. She's become immune to what happens on the dock. Glaring at her, I ask, "You have something to say?"

"Thank you."

"Good. Now get the fuck out of here. You have less than five minutes." That's all the warning she's going to get, and all she needs because she high tails it out of the area, limping and gripping her side.

If it had been any other circumstance, I would have been kinder and offered aid, but revenge has turned my blood cold, and there's no room for kindness now.

Stepping up to his lifeless body, I kick the fucker. Smiling, I drop down and snatch the watch off his wrist. The piece of shit stole the gift my mother had given to my father on their first anniversary.

The leather has been worn and replaced once over the years, but the inscription is still there. *I loved you from our first meeting.* I wrap it up in a handkerchief and tuck it into my pocket to be cleaned and put away.

His father will have all the proof it was me in due time, but we don't need to linger.

"We better head out before any more of his guards

appear. The rest of the civilians have been warned to evacuate."

I planned my attack with the least amount of casualties and there are a lot less people around here today. With the river icing over, the pier gets pretty lifeless this time of year except those who aren't supposed to be here. The deals done in the dark will be put on hold for the time being because I've destroyed their meeting place.

Five minutes after we pull away, rows of explosions are set off. Destroying a large portion of Volchek's property and sending their stolen goods into the icy Neva River while still leaving Junior's body to be found as I left him. The explosives worked perfectly.

Knowing that this property is owned by one of the bratva, the police will be careful to avoid getting involved unless requested. It's the one thing I do have to love about corruption. There's always someone willing to take cash to forget they saw anything, and thirty more too afraid to say a word.

"One down. So many more to go before we get him."

"He's going to strike soon," Alek says.

That is, without a doubt, a reality I'm begging for, but I feel down in the depths of my soul that Volchek is a natural coward, and he'll wait until he thinks he has the upper hand, which he won't.

"Yes, he will, and I look forward to it. Let us get some lunch. For the first time in days, I actually have an appetite." A smile spreads over my friend's face. I know he's been worried about me and I can't blame him, but my will was too strong to let myself fade away without vengeance.

Since the death of my parents and little brother, food has been the last thing I wanted and only I bothered to consume it to keep my strength. I've spent the past week working out daily for hours, training in the cold, and getting ready for the war to come my way.

"Sounds good." Alek rubs his flat stomach. Like most of my men, we all stay extremely conditioned, but a good meal is hard to pass up, especially in the cold.

As we drove to the house Alek informed my cook to start my meal. When we arrived, the housekeeper greeted us. "Sir, your lunch will be ready in ten minutes."

"Very good, Angelina. Have it brought into my office when it's ready."

"Yes, sir." She nods and leaves us as we head down the hall and into my office to discuss the next round of attacks. Other pressing matters need my attention, especially my legal businesses. However, I can't seem to focus on anything other than the blood that needs to be spilled. Most believe that I'm in the grieving stage and therefore taking leave. Although I must admit that my grief will forever linger inside my soul, that isn't the reason I'm neglecting my work.

I slide the manila folder out of the thumbprint locked drawer in my desk. It's everything Drago sent me on my next target.

"I will get her tonight." My mind goes straight to Katya Volchek and the fact that she's been a secret that he's kept for nineteen years. A prize he's kept locked away like a greedy king, but he messed up, and the bratva prince knows just where to find her. A smile spreads over my face like a sick and twisted vulture.

"Roman, I know it's not my place or anything, but she's innocent in all of this." Fire burns in my guts and shines through my eyes as I look at him.

Calmly, I sit back in my chair and say, "You're right,

Alek. It isn't your place. I know very well what part she's had to play in any of this, but this isn't about her. This is about what I can do to destroy him. Ilya was truly innocent." If there's anyone who had been pure, it had been him and that didn't stop Volchek.

There is a knock at the door, and it's the food. "Here you are, sir. If you need anything else, Maria said she can have it prepared quickly."

"No, thank you. This will do." She leaves us again, closing the door behind her. See, that's the kind of help I like. They do their job and don't question me at all, unlike this asshole.

"Forgive me. You are right." He will placate me because he knows it will please me, but it's not true. Alek has never been a good liar, and that's why he makes for a great friend.

I chuckle. "Do not bullshit me, Alek. You don't agree with my decision, but you said you'd be by my side on this." Getting serious, I straighten up in my chair. I ask, even though I know the answer, "Has that changed?"

"No. I just don't want you to regret becoming just like him." I looked at my lunch, having lost my appetite again. I stab the meat violently, trying to avoid the whole fucking moral debate.

"Katya Volchek will be dealt with. End of story. Now eat and shut your yap, so I can attempt to enjoy the cook's effort."

"It does smell fantastic."

"You will get no arguments here." We dig into our lunch, and with his silence, I can finally savor every bite.

We're halfway done with our food when he asks, "Do you think he's gotten the message yet?"

"Yes." My phone takes that moment to ring. Looking at

the ID, I sent it to voicemail because I won't let my meal get cold. "He most definitely knows." I chuckle.

"Your cook is incredible. It's just not fair." He rubs his flat stomach like somehow he's normally deprived of a good meal.

"Sorry, my friend, but you eat here every day, so I doubt you have much to complain about, no?" I remind him that essentially my cook has been his cook for years.

"I suppose you have a point." He chuckles, taking another bite of food. We continue to eat as my phone goes off with several messages. None of them are important at the moment, and no more from Vladimir.

"Shall we begin the next stage?" Alek asks, setting his plate down on my desk.

I check my watch and decide that I had two hours before I had to prepare for the takedown. "How about some pool for now?"

"Let's go. I need to trounce you in something."

"You can try." We set our plates on the waiting cart outside my office, and then I lock the door before we have some time to decompress. Rolling up my sleeves, I grab a pool cue while Alek racks up the table. We could play for hours and have before all my family had been destroyed. It brings me a semblance of peace, but I have matters than need to be dealt with. By the time we're done playing, I've beat him two games to one.

"I must prepare. Gather the men for a briefing before we depart." I run up to my room and change into a suitable outfit to greet my next target.

"It's time," Alek says, standing outside my bedroom door. My men are ready for the next part of the mission, which will happen soon.

"Here it is. We watch and wait. If anyone gets in our

way, we take them out, but we're not moving until I give the signal. Does anyone have a question or a problem?" They shake their heads. "No one touches little Princess Katya. She's mine to deal with. Understood?"

"Yes, boss," a chorus of voices say. Despite what Alek might have believed, I wasn't going to kill her, but I wanted her to suffer. Holding her prisoner sounded like a great idea, but I hadn't considered what I'd do with her once my revenge against her father came to an end.

"Let's go and make Volchek pay." The drive to her hidden location is an hour and a half away. We break off, taking different ways to get there to avoid drawing attention since the area is extremely remote.

My group arrives first because I want eyes on her before anyone else. Given that she's been well-guarded, there are no known images of her. With all of our surveillance, they couldn't get a clear image of her over the past week and a half.

With my binoculars, I get my first visual of the little princess.

Fuck…. Not fucking okay.

Barely taller than the broom in her hands, her slender figure twirls in the middle of her kitchen, and I've never seen anything more beautiful. With nearly icy blond hair braided down her back, Katya spins as she smiles without care. She's listening to headphones and I want to know what song has her so joyous and unaware. She has no idea that her father has put this target on her back, and I never miss.

My men are used to waiting, so they are calm, but I've suddenly felt the weight of every minute that ticks by. I'm not bothered by the cold; I've never felt warmer than I am now, but I won't let any attraction I feel dissuade me from my mission. Even as the attraction builds to the point of pain between my legs in the frigid, frosty night.

Watching the enchanting fairy move around, I almost miss the woman coming into the house. She yells at the young girl, taking the broom from her and then swings it over her ass, striking her backside. Katya yelps, choking back the tears as she drops her head, and I just found my first kill for the night.

My anger blooms so deep in my head that I miss the rest of what's said. "That bitch dies."

We stay in the periphery until the signal is given. Loading an explosive under the woman's car, I climb right back onto my perch and wait.

My phone rings as hers does. It's the call I've been waiting for. "Answer it, Princess," I whisper from my perch in the low trees that hide her garden cottage.

"Katya." Volchek's voice is haggard and agitated.

"Daddy." God, her voice is like an angel. That shouldn't even be right.

"What have I told you?" he snaps at the young girl.

"Mr. Volchek, can I help you?" The broken tone makes me angry on her behalf. Bastard.

CHAPTER TWO

KATYA

MY WEEKLY VISIT from my evil nanny is over, and I can finally be alone. I breathe a sigh of relief as the door locks behind her. It's funny that I spend every single day alone, and I should be grateful for the company, but it's a torture I'd rather do without. She dropped off my groceries with the help of the one guard my father assigned to the cottage.

The guards change throughout the day. Not that it matters to me because they're not allowed to speak to me. They're just to ensure no one can get into the cottage, and I can't get out. You'd think I'd be able to leave now that I'm older, but it doesn't work that way.

Still, I'm glad she's gone because I can get back to cooking and cleaning for myself. My own company for a lifetime is better than being with her for even just one minute.

First things first, I head to my room, where my only two electronic devices are charged. Snatching up my headphones, I return to the kitchen and pick my tunes to enjoy while I cook and clean.

My stomach rumbles with hunger just thinking about what I'm making tonight. It's nothing special, but it's such a delicious soup. It will take an hour to make, but it's so worth it as the nights grow colder. Prepping the vegetables from my garden, I chop and rinse them before bringing them to a nice simmer with the small piece of meat.

As I wait for the kitchen to fill with the wonderful aroma, I get to cleaning.

I twirl around in my cottage to the music from my newest MP4 player I got for Christmas last year. Has it been that long already? Of course, it has. The colder air has gripped the area, and it is the end of October. I grab the broom that has seen better days. "Care to dance, good Sir?"

I press play and dance around the room like the old wood is my prince and feeling like Briar Rose without the nutty fairies or a wicked evil being out to get me.

Spinning around the kitchen as if it's a ballroom that I've only read about, I picture myself in the loveliest pink gown as the man of my dreams tells me I'm the one he wants to marry and have a family with. Goodness, even in my head I sound completely like her. suppose I'm more like her than a normal girl my age. I was orphaned and locked away because my father was afraid people would find out about me and use me to get to him, harming me or even worse.

My mother died in childbirth, and I was quickly sent to this cottage before I cut my first tooth because I'd almost been kidnapped. They were never triumphant again, but I feel I lost out on a family because of it. I've lost out on life anyway, living out here all alone without someone to spend time with me. Maybe that's why he's never acted like a real father to me, or what I believe a father should be. My only references to parents were from the books that I've read.

I've never owned a television, so books have been my only outlet to the real world until I got my music player which has been a blessing. I didn't know I was missing it in my life, and a part of me wants to know what else is out there, outside of these crumbling walls, and the wooded forest. I've fallen in love with so much music that it keeps me from going insane most days. According to my nanny, most of the music is old, but it's really good, so I don't care.

A band called The Beatles plays in my ears, and they're probably one of my favorites. I dance to *While My Guitar Gently Weeps*, and I find happiness.

Suddenly, I'm caught off guard, and Olga comes back into the cottage. She snatches the broom from my hands and then catches me on the ass, swatting me with the handle. The quickness of her attack always gets me, and I'm never prepared for it, but I bite back the pain. The bruising will last for a week, and there's nothing I can do about it. My father tells me it's the lesson I need to learn, and I'd stop getting beat when it sinks in.

I thought Olga was gone for the week, and I wouldn't see her again for another one, but maybe I should have been a bit more cautious and waited to see her drive away.

With her over-jeweled fingers, she slams the curtains shut and starts shouting. "Have you lost your mind, you dumb girl?" she yells in English because even though I was born and raised in Russia my entire existence, they never taught me anything but English. I rub my hand over my backside, hoping to stop some of the pain from spreading, but it doesn't help. It burns and I'm sure I'll have a massive mark on my bottom, making it hard to sit for days.

"You're useless, and if your father didn't pay me to keep you alive, I'd kill you, myself." She yanks my headphones down, sending my player to the floor, stepping on it. My heart cracks with the device. Every word from her mouth cuts sharper than before and there's a new sense of anger building in me.

"You broke my headphones."

"I'll do more than that if you don't learn to behave. There are people out there ready to steal you off, and you act like a foolish girl with dreams. They will never happen."

I've had enough of this woman who's been nothing but a plaything for my father when he does actually visit. "Then why am I here? If I'm trapped in a cottage with no future, I have better things to do with my life." My voice is raised and higher pitched than it's ever been as I feel like I'm going to just lose it.

"You will once your father has the highest bidder to take you." The snide comment slips past her lips as she adjusts her blouse.

"What?" I ask, finally ready to take control. Never have I heard anything about being someone's bargaining chip, an item for sale. Although it would make sense, I hadn't thought he'd be capable of that. They have taken my last piece of comfort and now this.

The anger on my face must show because she's quick to correct herself. "Oh, he's not putting you up for sale just yet, but he can't lose out on such a precious commodity. Why don't you think he's kept his guards out of the house with such prime meat in their faces all day? Young pussy goes for a lot of money."

Shaking my head, I narrow my eyes at this woman who has no regard for me in the least. "You just hate me so damn much. It makes no sense, so if you're done assaulting me, do you mind getting the hell out of my home?"

"I would, but I'm waiting for a call from your father." Or my brother. Olga would stick her claws in either of them if she could, but she'll never understand that she's just another woman to them.

"Looking for someone to screw that old pussy." I toss her disgusting words right back at her.

"You have a filthy mouth on you."

"I only learned it from the best." I look over at the knives in my chopping block and consider what would happen if I just stabbed this bitch. My father could easily find another whore to deliver groceries.

"Little girl, know your place." She slaps me across the face. I'm about to grab the large knife when my crappy cell phone rings. It only allows me to make a call to my father's number and doesn't have any internet. It's like a phone from before I was born.

"Katya," he says the second I answer.

"Daddy," I called him, hoping he'd hear the upset in my voice.

"What have I told you?" Of course, he doesn't, or he doesn't care.

Straightening my shoulders, I clear my throat and respond like the dutiful subject. "Mr. Volchek, can I help you?"

"Vlad has been killed, which means you're in danger." A gasp escapes my lips, but not for my brother. The threat is real, and that means someone could actually come after me. Although I can't see why.

"He's dead?" I question, pretending to care as I choke out my reply. My brother, if I can call him that, was worse than my father because he made his hatred for me clear as day.

He snarls and huffs before answering. "Yes, are you deaf, girl? I want you to take care to stay inside and keep all the doors locked until my team can get you out of the house safely." What would I do without such a lovely family? I'm not allowed to go outside, anyway. The garden is almost completely sheltered from the woods and a large walled enclosure.

"Your team? How will I know who they are?" It's not like I have a good relationship with these people.

"They have a code word. Aurora." I smile because it makes me feel like at least he understands me.

"Aurora. Okay," I repeat. Then I look at his trollop who is standing with her hand on her hip waiting for me to finish talking to my father. "What about your witch that's here?"

"She should have left already. Put her on the phone." He doesn't correct me this time which means things have gotten crazy in the real world.

"Cow, my father wants to talk to you." I pass the outdated phone to her.

"Yes, Sir. Yes. Roman Semyonov. Okay. I'm departing now. I'll warn the guards to be on the lookout."

"Be gone, witch. I have to prepare to leave." I grin and wave her off.

"One of these days, you're going to pay for that mouth of yours."

"You get paid with that mouth of yours. Now, since I

actually have a threat coming after me, and you're going to be useless, please leave before I get the urge to practice my self-defense on you." I grab the kitchen knife and point it in her face. The urge to use it on her is very real. My brother is dead and someone's after me, standing up for myself feels good and right.

She eyes me with the dirtiest look before leaving and locking the door behind her. For a brief moment I feel a rush of power I've never had before.

Smiling, I peek through the curtains and watch her pull away. Olga doesn't get more than the driveway when her blue car explodes. I fall back in shock, letting out a scream as I hit the floor and the knife sliding under the table.

"Oh my God," I cry out, crawling off the floor in a hurry.

I rush upstairs to my bedroom and grab my things, slipping on my best shoes and head back downstairs just as the door bursts open. I'm stunned in place at the sight of a hulking man in a dark suit with two men behind him. His eyes meet mine and I see the darkness in the light honey colored eyes. I'm staring at the most handsome and dangerous man I ever saw. The deadly look in his eyes both scares and arouses me.

"Thank goodness, I thought we were too late, Princess Katya." He dusts off the snow on the top of his shoulders and steps over the busted door.

"Who are you?" He's got to be a giant, and his face is bare of facial hair, but I can see the dark shadow starting to fill in. His looks have me captivated that I almost miss what he says.

"Your father sent me in to move you to a safe location. We just saw your nanny's car explode as we pulled up."

"What's the code word?" I ask with my hands on my waist, holding the knife at my side.

He stalks closer to the steps unafraid of the blade in my hand. With a cool confidence he says, "Aurora." The way it rolls off his tongue, I want to rush into his arms.

"That's right." My voice is just a whisper as I continue to stare. Another man appears from behind him and whispers something.

"Now, let's hurry before the man who came to kill you appears to get the job done." My eyes move to the open doorway and the fire burning outside.

Panic sets in when after all the years of threats and warnings my father drilled into my head is finally real. "Why would anyone want to kill me? I no one knew about me."

"Some secrets can't be kept hidden." He steps forward and snatches the knife from my hands, and I gasp. Everyone is so much quicker and tougher than me.

"Hey, that's for my protection."

He scoffs, tossing it into the sink. "You could cut yourself. Where is your coat?"

I pulled it out of the closet. "This is the only one I have." Sliding it on, I forgot the zipper doesn't work anymore, and it doesn't matter because I can't close it, anyway. It's nice, but it's clearly old and doesn't quite fit my adult body anymore.

His eyes move to the middle of my chest where my hand attempts to hold the coat closed. My shape has changed as my breast grew, but my father and brother didn't care because I never left except to go to the back garden. That reminded me about my food on the stove.

"My soup," I exclaimed. One of the men with him goes to the pot and lifts the lid, breathing in my food.

"It smells incredible." It brings a grin to my face. No one has ever given me a compliment before.

A low growl comes from beside me. I hadn't realized how close he was standing next to me. "Leave it, Alek," my hero barks out.

My hero peels off his overcoat and throws it over my shoulders. It smells like freshly fallen snow and his masculine scent. I don't know if it's a cologne like the guards and my father wear, but it's nice. "We don't have time for anything else." He leads me out of the house, refusing to wait for my objections.

"I left my phone back there," I say, trying to keep up with his large strides.

"That dinosaur will be fine. Your father will contact me soon after we get you to a safe place," he says without stopping his broad frame trudging through the snow.

"Thank you. It's a big risk and so dangerous, whoever this guy is. He killed my brother."

"I know. Katya, I'm not afraid," he says with a chuckle and confidence that I've only read about. I hope he's right. They open the door and freeze. "Inside, now." I look back at the still-burning car.

"It's safe. I promise." He nudges me inside before he slides in behind me, and the car just got a lot warmer, so I'm sure I don't need his coat anymore. I'm about to pull it off when he stops me. "Leave it on."

I nod, following his orders because there's just something about him that's commanding. I never enjoyed following the orders from the other men my father hired. Something is different about him or maybe it's the new situation of being in danger.

We pull away, and he says, "See. You're safe."

We get out of the long path, a place I've never been

before. We make it onto the road when we are suddenly being shot at. I scream and cling to him. "Off me, Katya." He shoves me to the vehicle's floor while the men in the car lower the windows and open fire on the cars that came after us.

I hear gunfire all around me, and I cling to the coat while I hide under his legs, hoping this all goes away. Moments later, it's all over, and he's lifting me off the floor and back into my seat like nothing happened.

My father must have some amazing men who work for him because they get rid of the guys after me.

"They got here fast," the one he called Alek says.

"Not fast enough," my hero answers with a smirk.

"That was close. I hope you're not hurt." I look up at my hero, running my hands over his upper body. and check for injuries, but he shakes his head.

He takes my hands and removes them from his body. "No, Princess. I'm fine. Now let's get you to safety." *Silly girl, don't fall in love with the first nice guy you meet.*

CHAPTER THREE

ROMAN

TWO THINGS ARE VERY clear to me. She has no self-preservation, and she has no feelings for her brother. When the shots came flying, I felt a strange emotion and had to protect this naïve girl. She looked up at me like I hung the moon, and I will destroy that shit soon. For now, I'm going to enjoy the pleasure of her soft, bright blue eyes on me while she thinks of me as her savior.

My men remain silent for the drive, shooting me several glances as Katya clings to me. Fuck, why does it feel so good to have her on me like this? We remain quiet so she doesn't catch on that we're not the rescue team she was expecting. We make the drive back faster because we're all ready to get to safety. The sound of a tiny rumble comes from her stomach which echoes loudly in the silence.

"Are you hungry?" I ask as we get closer to my compound.

"Yes, but I'm not sure if I could eat after everything

that's happened." Tears are in her eyes, and Alek's words hit harder than before. I'm not a monster like Vlad, but I have a mission, and I have an interest in this beauty that forced a change in my plans, if only a little.

She begins to shiver by my side, and I realize she's in shock. Sliding my arm around her, I rub her shoulder. Katya snuggles in close, nestling up to me like I'm her protector. "You're going to be okay." But will I? My head and heart are fucking playing a tug of war that isn't for the faint of heart.

We arrive at my home and find it ready for us with hot food for my men. "Let me show you to your room, and I'll have your food brought up."

"I can't eat with everyone else?" I feel like a dick, but that's not going to happen.

"It wouldn't be proper." More like I have things to discuss with them.

"Okay," she says, her voice broken. She slides off my coat, and her pebbled nipples are visible through her worn pale blue dress.

"Tomorrow, we'll see. Okay. Besides, you're not dressed for dinner."

"Sorry, I don't have nice clothes." She slaps her hand to her mouth, knowing that she probably shouldn't have said something negative about her father. Not that I give two fucks about that lowlife, but I've learned a lot about Katya's life that wasn't in the file. His men had been treated with more respect and decency than she had.

"It's not that." My eyes move down to her chest. She follows my gaze.

"Oh, my goodness. I'm so...." Her pale face reddens like a delicious apple I want to sink my teeth into.

Slipping my fingers under her slender chin, I tip her

head to meet my gaze. "Don't be embarrassed in front of me. In front of my men, it's unacceptable. Let me escort you to your room."

The embarrassment fades, but then I see that look again. The same one she gave me the moment I used the code word. *Desire.*

Fuck, I send up a silent prayer that I can figure this all out, and soon.

Taking her hand, sending tendrils of pleasure through me, I lead her up the stairs to my bedroom. Everything is securely locked, so she can't get out or find the code to the guns, but I've decided she won't stay in the dungeon after all. My bedroom is her new home. She'll get used to it, and so will I. My cock jerks in my slacks, beating against the tight boxers and stretching the fabric.

"Wow, this room is beautiful and bigger than my entire cottage." She looks around and notices the masculine things while I take the time to adjust my pants.

"Oh my goodness. Is this a television?" She spins on her weathered heels to look back and forth between me and the TV. I don't think I've ever been jealous of an inanimate object until this girl.

"Yes." My voice is hoarse for some reason, so I clear it and repeat myself. "Yes."

"I've never seen a television before." She slaps her hand on her mouth.

"What?"

Her face scrunches up before she asks, "Maybe if it's not too much trouble, I could watch it while I'm here." The light in her eyes makes her entire face brighten up, and it's beautiful.

I can't believe she's never seen one before. If she keeps looking at me like that, she can have one in every damn room in the compound. "I'll get it set up for you, but I'm not sure you'll find much to watch. What do you do for fun?"

"I read books from authors like Jane Austen, Charles Dickens, and Aesop's fairytales." Nodding, I search for a movie while my brain tries to process what she just revealed. Are you fucking kidding me? What did he expect her to do? I turn on the television and select Pride and Prejudice in Russian.

"Your dinner will be brought up shortly." I don't think I'm strong enough to bring it up myself without kissing the fuck out of her.

"Thank you again. I don't know your name."

"Roman." Her brows knit, and then she adjusts them as if she's heard my name before. I remember Vlad mentioning it to Olga on the phone. Shit, have I ruined the plan?

"Thank you, Roman." She slips off her worn shoes and sits on the edge of the bed, looking like a goddamn pauper on my nice sheets. Stealing one last look, I close the door. Vlad's got a lot of explaining to do before I kill him.

I head downstairs and warn the men in the hall to stay away from my room. Alek is the first to look at me with a grin splitting his face. "Karma, my friend."

"Shut up. My plans haven't changed. Vlad will pay, and she will be a part of it."

"You'd hurt that adorable little kitten?" His tone doubted that I could kill her. It's true, though. One look and harming a hair on her head had become impossible. I never intended on killing her but making her life hell had been my plan. Now that seemed unbearable to me. She looked like she'd already lived in hell and the devil had been her father.

"No, but I will do something else. He took my family, so I'll take his.... and make it mine." The thought of breeding her had been on my brain the second I caught her twirling in the kitchen.

"Whoa. What?" Alek's eyes widen, mouth falling open like a slack jawed fool.

"She will be carrying the next line of Semyonov sons."

"Good luck, my friend." He claps my shoulder and shakes his head.

"You doubt my ability to breed her."

"No, that's not something I doubt, but when your revenge is over and your bride is crushed, will she come to you willingly?" *Fucking asshole.* His wisdom is starting to work my nerves.

"No one asked your damn opinion, and you know nothing will stop me from killing Vlad."

"That I'm sure of. Steal her heart as well as her body, and then tell her to get in the kitchen and make that damn soup. It smelled so good." I whack him in the back of the head.

"Find your own bride."

"Maybe I will. How old is your cook?"

"Idiot." We head into the kitchen where my crew from tonight's raid are eating.

"Maria, please prepare two meals on trays." Although I should stay away from her, I just can't.

When I get a raised brow from Alek, I growl, "I have questions for her."

She set up two trays while I turned to my soldiers, who did their job effortlessly and effectively. "Men, I have decided my revenge on Vladimir Volchek will not be to kill his daughter. She's less valuable to him, but I will make her mine and destroy him that way. He was planning to sell her off. The same rules apply. You are only to speak to her if necessary, and you are most definitely not allowed to touch her in any way. If I catch your hands or eyes lingering on her, you will lose them. Understood?"

There is a chorus of affirmatives. "Yes." Now that that's settled, a little tension slides off my shoulders.

Taking our dinner upstairs, I have my guard open the door and find Katya sitting on the edge of the bed, biting her bottom lip. She turns to look at me with bright eyes and a smile. "You're back." Fuck, that melts the icy shroud just a bit.

"I thought we could have food together."

"That would be nice. I never eat with anyone except my brother and father. Well, it only happens once in a while. I shouldn't say anything." Panic strikes her entire body, and then I remember the bitch whooping her ass inside the cottage. "Please don't say anything to him. I don't want to get in trouble." Her back is ramrod stiff as if she's afraid of being hit again.

I set the food down on the table for the times I do have a meal in my room, and then I walk over to Katya and sit beside her on the bed. "Don't worry about him. I'm not letting him harm you just because you were clearly neglected."

"You're so kind to me." Tears fall from her eyes, forcing me to pick her up in my arms and sit her on my lap.

"I didn't mean to cry," she sobs in my arms. "It's been a long day."

I brush the loose strands from her face. "Let's get you fed and in bed."

"Is this your room?" Her eyes are asking more than one question.

"It is."

"Where are you going to sleep?" Buried between your thighs.

"Right beside you. I promised to protect you from my enemies." I take her hand and lead her over to the table and farther away from the bed so I don't lose my fucking mind. She has no idea what her beauty and sweet nature are doing to me, let alone the fact that I can almost see through that old gown.

"Okay." We eat quietly while I do my best to control the multitude of thoughts racing through my head. In an effort to find a distraction, I turn my attention to the television, and I realize how low the volume is, so I grab the remote and turn it up.

"Oh, that's fine. You didn't need to turn it up." She blushes like it took any effort for me to raise the volume.

Her fear of being a burden grates my nerves, and I let my temper slip. "Not everything is a chore, Katya." I'm not mad at her but at her situation.

"It's not that. I don't speak Russian." I stare at her like a fool, mouth hanging open. How is a woman who has been trapped in the heart of the forest in the middle of Russia not speaking the language?

"I know. I'm Russian, and I can't speak it or read it." She sets her fork down on the plate, frustration pouring off her as her lips purse.

"I'm sorry."

"No, I'm sorry. You've been wonderful, and I'm here acting like a baby because my normally secluded life isn't what everyone would expect."

"Don't be upset. We can get you a tutor." It's a promise I can easily keep. "Now eat."

She finishes her bite and tilts her head. "How long am I going to be here?"

The thought of letting her go is unfathomable, and it won't happen. Forever is the answer. "Until the threat has passed."

"Do you think it would take a long time?" Forever.

"I can't say. All I know is that you've had enough negative thoughts. Finish up, and let's get you to sleep."

"You're not going to join me." Anger hits me right in the chest. She's naïve as fuck, and there have been guards around her all the time.

"What do you know of men?" I ask, stabbing my fork into the dish a little more violently than necessary. The thought of them putting their filthy hands on her soft, tender skin sends me into a murderous rage.

"Only what I've read in those books and the warnings my father and Olga gave me." I can't have this conversation right here, so I pick her up from the chair and carry her into the bathroom.

I grip her face, holding it in my rough hands. "Do your father's other men come into your room and sleep in your bed?"

Her eyes widened, and her mouth gaped in shock. "Heavens no. They're not allowed to be in the house for more than a moment if they need to relieve themselves in the downstairs bathroom."

"That's smart of them because, Princess, I've decided that you can't go back. You're mine." My mouth lands on her, and her unpracticed lips freeze for just a moment until she melts against me. "Open your mouth." I take my tongue and slide it along hers, causing the sexiest moan to escape her.

"That's why I'll wait until you're asleep."

I release her face, but then she grabs onto my dress

shirt. "He'll kill you. No one is supposed to even talk to me."

Smiling down at her, I brush my knuckle under her chin. "Princess, he won't do a damn thing to me. I have to make a call, and you need to get in the shower. I'll get you something to wear. When I get back, you better be sleeping, or I'll forget all about your naivety and show you what you've been missing."

"Oh goodness." I adjust my cock and then turn on the shower behind me.

"I'm not good, but I'll give you all that I have in me." Leaning down, I brush my lips on her forehead and then excuse myself and quickly leave the bathroom. Pulling out a pair of boxers and a tee shirt, I set them on the bed.

Ivan is waiting at the bottom of the steps for me. "He knows you have her."

"I expected as much. Does he have his men circling their wagons outside?" I'm ready to go out there, guns blazing, if they even attempt a siege. However, I doubt that will be necessary. One thing about Volchek is his own self-preservation and not that of his family. His empire means everything, which is why he butchered my family.

He shakes his head, bringing up the footage on a security tablet, showing me the bastards lurking. "I spotted a few in the distance, but they're just monitoring it appears. I don't know what their angle is."

"Don't kill them. Have them brought to me. Enough with the games and wasting my time. Volchek will get his dues much sooner than I planned." I have a beautiful creature that deserves my attention.

"What about his daughter?" He's a great systems tech, but this is not his business.

"I thought I made my intentions clear."

"I don't mean that, Sir. I don't mean to pry, but we weren't prepared for her arrival, and she will need things. I have three sisters, and the amount a girl needs just to get through their day is insane." Damn, he's right, and it's not like I can take her out to pick whatever she wants.

"Thank you. Please send your sisters out with security to purchase attire for Katya. Elegant and comfortable clothes. I will get her sizes and give them an expense account. They can even buy themselves a few items for their efforts."

"Oh no. I'll just escort them and keep that bit to myself. They're not to be trusted with money when shopping for clothes."

I smirk. I have no idea what sisters are like, but I remember that my mother would love to go shopping and spend a great deal of money, buying clothes for herself and for us. "Very well. I must check on matters, so have this handled first thing in the morning."

"Yes, Boss." I head into my office and think about my next moves while they apprehend the pieces of shit lingering on my property.

Ten minutes later, my guys have them bagged and in the cellar, waiting on me to deal with the trash. I roll up my sleeves and grab a few weapons for a little fun. It's been a bit too easy and clean lately since I've invested my time into making money. A sick part of me didn't know how much I missed this until I took out the first guy on the wharf. Now, the thrill of the kill is back and deep in my bones.

Two guards stand outside the room while I hear the rat bastards shouting at Ivan in Russian about how we're all going to die. I chuckle as I get closer because it's so fucking cute, but the next words I overheard were too much for me to hold back. My expression changes and so does my humor. I burst through the door and pulled out my blade, putting it to the fucker's throat. The other guy is barely conscious in the back, face battered.

"You were there?" I ask, daring him to repeat what I overheard. There will be no mercy tonight.

The bastard has the nerve to look unbothered and unafraid as he answers, "Yes, and I listened to them scream like a baby." I swipe my blade along his knuckles, fileting them wide open.

"Good, because you will scream." I turn to Alek, who brings the salt. "I don't even need information anymore, Alek. Do I?"

"Nyet, Boss." I pour the salt, smirking as the bastard wails like a little bitch. Howling as the sting intensifies with each granule of salt.

"Music to my ears," I say. The torture I bestow is nothing compared to what he deserves for his words alone. He dared to bring more pain to me; reminding me of the horrors that my little brother suffered was a foolish thing to do. Nothing about it was brave, and now he'll suffer a much longer death, and I won't have an ounce of regret.

"Stop, please," he pleads like the pathetic weakling he truly is.

"Nope. Your balls are gone now, aren't they? You talked about butchering my family and dare ask that I show you a crumb of mercy? No, you will die slowly and painfully." I continue my torture, slicing his kneecaps and repeating the seasoning. "My dogs may enjoy the taste of seasoned meat a little more."

"How about this asshole?" I say aloud although I'm not directing it to anyone in particular.

I turn my attention to my other captive and ask, "What do you have to say?"

"Your father crossed Volchek and didn't hand over property Volchek demanded was his. Semyonov said it belonged to his family, so Vlad took their lives."

"How many were there?"

"Twenty men. Most of them died fighting the guards, but it was already too late for your father's men. Volchek and his small team had isolated them and attacked."

"Why are you telling me this?" I question him.

"I want my soul clean before I die." The conviction in his eyes is real. He has resigned himself to his fate which is wise because there is no other way out.

"Say your prayers." He does, and then I pull the trigger. No mercy.

I turn to the one with the big mouth and little balls. "Now you.... where was I?"

"Oh, God."

"No God here. The devil is all you get." I continue cutting him until he passes out for the third time.

"Roman, maybe we should call it a night and let him recover for now?"

As we head out, I give my guards on duty instructions. "Sounds good. Keep the fucker alive. I'll be back tomorrow." I need to go upstairs and see the one piece of Volchek that I plan on keeping.

CHAPTER
FOUR

ROMAN

I ENTER the bedroom as quietly as possible, but it's not enough because she's still wide awake and on the bed in my shirt and boxers with her legs crossed.

"Everything okay?" she asks, looking up at me with such adoration, and I'm about to destroy it soon.

"Yes, I just have to take a shower. Get under the covers, and I'll be out in a minute." I close the bathroom door and strip out of my slightly bloody clothes before turning on the spray. Not needing to wait for it to warm, I wash off the blood and filth of the day.

When I get to the heavy meat between my legs, I groan. The fucker won't stay down around her. It's better that I get one out now before climbing in bed and taking her virginity right now when I'm so fired up. Stroking it from base to tip, I think about that little beauty spread out on my bed, naïve and eager to learn the things she was never taught. My hand tightens around my length while the other grips the wall.

Growling, I imagine her tiny hands wrapping around my girth, learning how to please me before she drops to her knees and sucks on my cock. Taking this fat fucker between those soft lips, struggling to take inch after inch. The vision is overwhelming and my orgasm shoots through me like a bolt of lightning. I roar, sending my load onto my shower floor as I belt out her name. I wash off my mess, and as I do, I hear the sound of someone trying the doorknob.

"Is everything okay? I can't get in there. The door is locked," she says in a panic.

I turn off the jets and wrap a towel around my waist before opening the door. "I'm fine, Princess. It's locked… for a good reason."

The sight of her expression is one that I'll keep in my head forever. "You're naked." Her hand comes to her mouth as she stares with wide eyes.

"That usually happens when you take a shower. However, you're mistaken." With a tug of my towel, I let it fall to the floor. "Now, I'm naked." Her gaze moves south and lingers on my cock, which enjoys the admiration a little too much and stands at attention.

"Oh my… it's huge." She bites down softly on the side of her bottom lip. The innocent modesty is there, but so is the excitement, and I'm going to test those waters right now.

Closing the distance between us, I grip the nape of her neck. "I told you to go to sleep, little girl. It looks like you're going to get that first lesson."

"I feel like I've had several lessons already. It makes sense why my dad kept his men away from me. I'm surprised we've never met before. I wouldn't have forgotten you."

My mouth is on hers as I lift her up and carry her off to bed, laying her down while I press my body onto hers. There's no waiting because the war is only starting, and I need to be inside her before she learns the truth.

My hand fists her blonde hair, gripping it tightly as I ask the question burning in my chest. "Did you want the others to fuck you, Princess?" I need her to give me the right answer.

"No, of course not, but I feel something inside when you look at me." The answer calms down the beast inside, but then she runs her soft hands up my chest, and a new animal has awakened.

Releasing my hold on her, I skim my hand down her throat and ask, "Where, baby girl? Tell me where you feel it." She blushes, innocence keeping her from giving me a verbal reply, so I'll coax it out of her.

"Here," I asked, cupping her tits. She moans, but I'm not even close to getting my desired answer.

"Here?" I slide my hand lower under the boxers, touching her wet curls.

"Roman," she moans my name, and I'm done for.

"That's because you know you belong to me." I slip my hand from her treasured slit and drag her shirt over her head, tossing it somewhere on the floor. My mind is focused on getting her naked, and that's all that matters. "Lift your hips, baby girl." She does, and I slide down the boxers.

"So, fucking sexy. Are you ready for me to teach you your next lesson?" I ask, watching her war between heated needs and her innocent fears. "Answer me, Katya."

"Yes, please." I drop my head and suck on her tiny pink nipples, stiffening them as I grab onto her massive chest. Soon they'll be enlarged and ready to feed our baby, but for now, they're mine to play with. She softly whimpers, parting her lips; I lift my eyes to watch her face. She's lost in the pleasure like a very good girl.

"Open those gorgeous eyes; I want you to see what I'm doing to you, Princess." She does and gasps as my hand finds her tight hole.

"Roman." Her voice shakes as I massage one finger into the untouched entrance.

"Time for another lesson." I lower down to my stomach, sandwiched between her thighs with my face right on her tiny cunt. With a slight brush of my tongue on her folds, she bucks. "Relax. I want you to pass the assignment, Princess." Sliding my tongue over her clit while I pump and stretch my finger as deep as I can, I listen to the soft cries grow louder.

"Something's happening," she says, her voice shaking as much as her thighs. My eyes steal as many glances as possible at the sight before me.

"Let it, baby girl. Come for me." She does, coming on my tongue, hips rolling as she shouts my name from her lips.

"That was beautiful."

"Did I pass?" she asks, looking for my approval.

"Yes, so perfect, but we're not done." My cock lines up at her entrance. "I need you to relax for me and trust me. Can you do that for me?"

"Yes, Roman," she says, nodding with such trust in her gorgeous icy blue eyes. They shine so brightly with lust.

I fist her hair in my hand, attempting to gain control as I push my thick tip through her tight pussy. "It's going to hurt, but it will be over soon." Before she can respond, I slam my big dick deep into her womb, claiming her.

She cries out, but I cover her screams with my lips.

Slowly she allows my kiss, opening her mouth and letting my tongue dance with hers. "The pain is almost over, and then I'll make it better."

"It's too big."

"It will be fine. You'll get used to me being inside your tight hole because it was made for me to take over and over." I kiss her and start to slide in and out, watching her face until the look of pain fades with every thrust.

Once she's with me, I increase my pace until she's ready to come again. Dragging my lips along her throat, I suck on her, marking my territory just a bit before returning to those plump tits that are starved of attention.

Her hands are in my hair, running them down to my shoulders. "That's it; touch me, baby girl." She intensifies her hold, and then I lose it, slamming into her while crushing her lips with mine. Seconds pass before both of us come. My cum sprays her walls as I hold still inside her, ensuring I coat them well. We have a family to make.

Our kisses continue even after the passion between our legs has stopped shaking, but if I don't pull out now, I won't get out of her ever again. She feels too incredible. My cock is throbbing back to life. Slipping out of her warmth isn't something I'm a fan of.

"I liked that lesson a lot, Roman."

"Good." I look down and see her blood on my cock. A bit of me feels triumphant, but then I remember that my Princess is innocent in all this, and my revenge against her father will put a rift between us.

"Something wrong? Oh no. Did I do that?" I rapidly school my expression and then smile.

"No, baby girl. I did that when I took your innocence. That shouldn't happen again, and hopefully, the pain will lessen every time I take you."

"That would be nice." She blushes and ducks her head under the covers.

It's so fucking sexy and adorable that I can't resist. I pull them away and pounce on her. "Don't hide from me." Kissing her fiercely, I add, "Let's get you washed up and ready to go back to bed."

"Yes, Sir." She salutes me, and I scoop her up, which causes her to flinch. The mirror gives me a view of her backside as we enter the bathroom.

"What's on your ass?" That's when I noticed the bruise from that bitch earlier.

"It's nothing."

"Nothing?" I already knew the answer, but I wanted her to tell me. I want to hear everything she has to say.

"Well, before you arrived, my nanny guard punished me for having the curtains open."

"Now, I'm not even a bit sorry that she died in that explosion. She shouldn't have dared touch you —ever." I drop down and kiss her back where the bruises have formed.

"You're too good to me, Roman."

"I'm always going to try to be that way." My fingers dip into her sopping wet cunt from behind.

"Do you promise?" she asks, losing her voice as I strum her clit.

"Forever." As I pull her into the shower, my mouth is on hers with my one hand still pumping her pussy until she's crying out my name again.

It's late when we both curl up on the bed, wrapped up in the covers. Not long later sleep overtakes her. There will be no sleep for me tonight. I have to be prepared for whatever Volchek has planned. He's been too damn quiet. The thought of him coming to get her sets my teeth on edge, so I have to strike sooner than I had scheduled. I've already wiped out half his men and a third of his businesses. Tomorrow the rest of the dominos will fall.

Everything depends on how strong his intent on is getting Katya back. I won't let it happen. Still, how far will he go to get his way?

Climbing out of bed, I dress in my pajamas and robe to go and check on the situation. Most of the house is in bed, but the night guards are there, keeping an eye on the perimeter.

I walk into the security room and check in with Ivan. "It's been quiet, except for his cries every once in a while. We have their electronics. They were communicating with Volchek's right-hand man, Anatoly Petrov's cousin, Abram."

"Petrov?" He hands me the report from the phones, and I read through the string of texts.

"Yes, according to the reports we've been getting in, he stopped working for his cousin a while back and then joined Volchek three days ago." The reports of Vlad's death and the wharf explosion have made the news, so it's time to give Volchek my condolences.

"Thank you. I have a call to make."

I leave him and head into my office, where I dial Volchek's secure line. "Vlad, it's good to hear you're still alive and kicking. I heard what happened at the wharf today. Terribly sorry about your loss."

"Fuck you, you bastard. I know it was you and I know you took my other prize. I want her back. She doesn't have a part in this and doesn't have to die for it." Wow, for a whole second, he actually sounds concerned. If I hadn't overheard their conversation, I might actually believe he cared.

"What prize?" The one I soiled with my seed, smiling to myself as I sat in my leather chair.

"Give her back to me." He sounds like a petulant child.

"I don't know who you're talking about," I answer with a hint of humor in my voice.

"My daughter."

"Since when do you have a daughter, Vladdy boy?"

"Bastard. You're asking for me to destroy you."

"Why? Were you looking to sell her off or hoping to give her to your next in line?"

"Your father got what he deserved by digging his nose into places it shouldn't have been. He wanted to take her from me, and now he's dead along with your family. I should have made sure to kill you as well."

"He'd been your friend. My mother and brother were innocent. Nothing can stop me from taking you down. I'll go keep an eye on the lovely little sleeping beauty. Or should I just call her Katya?" I end the call as he releases a bunch of curses.

What the fuck did he mean about my father wanting to take Katya away from him? I slam my fist down on the desk and then get up and pour a drink. Slamming it back, I go for another two more before I find myself too fucking angry, sending the glass into the fireplace.

Nothing in my plan changes for Volchek. Tomorrow, I'll clear out all his Eastern Shoreway shipping accounts. I want him squirming without the funds to attack me.

My next call is to Petrov. "Semyonov, it's three in the morning," he growls.

"Did you have something to do with my parents' deaths?" My question is direct.

"What? Are you fucking nuts? Of course, I wouldn't have shit to do with that."

"What does Abram do for you?"

"Abram and I have cut ties due to his behavior. He's an addict now and refuses to get help. I haven't seen him in weeks, but my people have told me he showed up at my corporate headquarters."

"I'm telling you I won't hold back and save any mercy for anyone involved with sending my brother into an early grave."

"I understand. You don't have a beef with me. Do what you must. However, I can't help you kill him. He's a piece of shit, but he's my family."

"As long as we understand each other. Do you know what's going on with Drago? I need to speak with him as well."

"He's busy in his own mess. He's got the daughter of a judge in his grasp, and I have a feeling the icy bastard has finally found someone to thaw that brutally cold heart of his."

"That's why he couldn't wait to get back home."

"Yes. I heard him talking to Polina about the girl's happiness in the home."

"Since when does that fucker care if anyone likes his home?"

"That's because he's got it bad."

"Thanks. I didn't think you'd have anything to do with everything, but Abram came up in my intel."

"I understand. Let me know if you need anything, Roman."

"I might take you up on it."

"Good. Now get some sleep. Some of us aren't in the middle of a war and have to get up and do real work."

"Asshole." I ended the call and felt better. These days it's too damn difficult to trust your own friends.

Turning off the lights, I head upstairs to where I really need to be. This time, my little sleeping beauty is curled up on my side of the bed with her face pressed into my pillow like she's trying to breathe me in.

I strip down to just my pajama bottoms and climb into bed, pulling her into my arms. She gasps and freaks out, arms flailing. "Calm down. It's just me."

"Sorry. This is new."

"Sleep." I brush my lips on the crown of her hair before tucking the covers around us and letting sleep take me too.

CHAPTER
FIVE

KATYA

I WOKE up to the most amazing feeling of being devoured by Roman. Opening my eyes all the way, I smile, knowing it's not a dream. "Good morning, sleeping beauty. I couldn't resist an early breakfast."

"Roman, it's like magic." I can't fight the orgasm as it hits me again. Until last night I had no idea what this part of life could be. Now I understand why Olga stayed around begging for my father and brother's attention.

"Is it always this good?" I ask, stretching as he climbs up my body.

"No, you're special." His mouth brushes along my throat, and then I feel his length against my stomach.

"What about you? Can I touch it?" I reach out my hand over his pajama pants.

"Go ahead, baby girl. I want you to get used to it." He closes his eyes as my hand runs along his length. It reminds me of his demand that I look at him while he gives me satisfaction. He's so lost in my touch that a low rumble rips through his chest, and he can't even abide by his own rules.

"Take me out." I follow his husky command, gripping the thick hardness and testing the smoothness between my fingers. It's so intense the way it jerks in my hand. I need more, so I rub it up and down, stroking the length. "Harder, baby girl."

My fist wraps around the massive girth, and I squeeze as I tug. "Fuck, you're going to make me nut."

"Is that bad?" His eyes fly open.

"No, nutting is all I can think about when you're around. Although I should save all my seed for between your legs where it belongs."

My heart rate picks up with every word from his lips. His golden eyes have darkened to a rich honey color, and I want to make him release any way he pleases.

"Then you should put it where it belongs," I challenged, wanting to be pummeled by his cock again.

He quickly flips me onto my back and growls while he presses his length against my hole.

"My little naïve Princess. You can't offer a man salvation so easily." He slams into me and kisses me roughly.

"You are my salvation," I confess, taking him inside me much easier than yesterday, even with the slight pain lingering. He rocks his hips, pumping faster into me.

"You have no idea what you're saying," he growls, sounding angry as he takes me violently.

"Yes, I do."

He starts whispering Russian in my ear, sending me over the edge. I drag his mouth to mine and bite his lip as my orgasm takes control of my body.

He growls and chuckles as he takes me harder,

thrusting his strong body into mine and pinning me into the luxurious mattress. Roman kisses me until I'm breathless and boneless.

I bite down on my bottom lip when I witness his taut muscles freeze over me. Roman comes, coating my womb until I can feel every ounce of the wetness of his release fill me up.

We kiss once more before he unceremoniously pulls out of me. "I need to get ready for work. You can stay in here until your clothes arrive, and then I'll take you downstairs to give you a tour of your new home."

"New home?" I sit up in the bed while he walks into the closet. "What about my father? Isn't he going to come to get me?"

He comes out and says, "Don't worry about that. The girls will be here with your clothes in a couple of hours."

"Girls?" A nagging feeling hits me, and his words start to bother me, *naïve princess*.

"Yes, I've had people go out and get you some new clothes." This is just too much, and I'm starting to panic. "Don't look upset, Princess." He cups my face, brushing my hair out of the way.

"Are they your lovers too?"

"No. I don't know them personally. They just know what a girl your age needs." He kisses me again. "Now, please shower and slide on some of my clothes before they come because I don't want anyone seeing you unclothed."

"Okay." He goes back to his closet, so I go to the bathroom and get cleaned up after relieving myself.

This is so insane, and even though I know my father's going to flip out when he finds out that his man has been inside me, I can't seem to care.

When I get out of the shower, my breakfast has been set

on the table, and *Pride and Prejudice* is on the screen, but it's in English this time. I stay in my robe with a towel in my hair as I eat my toast and jam, getting lost in the movie.

I've finished my breakfast when the door opens, and it's Roman. "You're still in your robe?"

"Sorry, I was so captivated by the movie and food." I instantly flinch, waiting for the anger to come out. He freezes and says, "Don't do that. Katya, I'm not going to hit you. It's fine since the girls have just arrived, and you'll have to try on what they bought to see if it fits."

"Okay."

"God, you're so beautiful. I'll just be downstairs, but if you need me, Alek will be right outside the door."

"Thank you."

"Give me a kiss, and that's all the thanks I need." I lift up on my toes and kiss his clean-shaven jaw. "Not good enough." He cups the back of my neck, spreading his fingers in my hair before laying those sexy lips on me. I melt in his arms, and he catches me before my knees buckle. The hand at my waist snakes under my robe grips my ass, and squeezes, bringing me against his full length.

"That was something else."

"Tell me about it, beautiful." He pats my bottom and then walks to the door, holding it open for three women who come in giggling with about half a dozen bags in each hand.

"All of this?"

"Please. That's just the first set." Two guards come in with more than double what they brought. They drop it all off and walk out without even looking in my direction. "There would have been more, but we didn't have a long time to shop."

I look up at Roman like he's lost his mind. I know he works for my dad, and he's super cheap, so he can't probably afford this. "I can't believe all of this is for me."

"Well, it is. I'll be downstairs." Roman kisses my temple and then leaves the room.

"So, let us see what we have here." One of the girls begins digging through the first bag, and another slaps her hands.

"Where are our manners? I'm Anna, this is Anya, and she's Mariska." She points to the one who had been digging in the bag.

"Do you work for Roman?"

"No. We're Ivan's sisters and here to help with whatever you need."

"They said you looked like the Ice Princess, so we thought these colors would look great on you." They pull out a bunch of gorgeous blues. Most of them are light-colored, and everything is nicer than anything I've owned.

"Wow, these are all beautiful."

"We have shoes for you too, but we weren't sure of your exact size. The ones you had were pretty worn, so we took a guess." They bring out several pairs and start sliding one after another on my feet without taking a break. Each one fits and is super cute.

"I told you these were perfect." They're a pair of fluffy white boots that look great even in my robe.

"How about we try on some of these clothes?" Anya says, shaking her head at her sisters.

"Oh, that would probably be a good idea. This is not very fashionable."

"I doubt Mr. Semyonov would care if it wasn't for all the men around here," Anna says, nodding and grinning.

"What do you mean?"

"You're gorgeous, and the man seems to be possessed." Anya slapped Mariska's arm, silencing whatever else she planned to say. Something in the pit of my stomach says things aren't adding up with Roman. Still, I go along with trying on the clothes.

I come out looking adorable in a pair of white and pale blue leggings, a pale blue long sweater that hangs off one shoulder, and the matching boots I'd tried on already. "Wow, could you look any cuter? You're hot and adorable at the same time. It's no wonder Mr. Semyonov can't stop checking in with Ivan."

"What do you mean?"

"Nothing. He's just asking how it's going with us up here."

"That's silly. I'm sure he's just doing his job for my dad." The mood shifts suddenly, and I don't know what it is, but then Mariska grabs the next outfit and demands I try it on before I get too cozy and forget the fashion show.

Their words linger in my head, but I begin to have so much fun that I forget all about it, and we laugh and giggle as I go from one outfit to another, feeling so pretty. After another hour, we're full of giggles and smiles, and the bed is a mess of clothes and shoes.

A knock at the door gets our attention.

"Come in," I call out. Roman enters looking sexy and haggard at the same time.

"How's it going?" he asks, staring straight at me.

"We were just finishing up, Sir," Anna answers.

"Thank you, girls. Your brother can escort you to your rooms for now."

"Our rooms?"

"Yes, you'll be staying with us temporarily. Some of your things will be here shortly."

"What's going on?" I ask. I like them, but there's no way I want three beautiful girls around my age getting to stay with Roman too.

"It seems that bringing them here has caught the notice of our enemies."

"Oh no."

"Your mother will be brought here now. Ivan went to get her and your things. Please let me have Alek show you to your room." They follow Alek out of the bedroom, and then Roman closes the door. I lost all the joy of the new clothes, knowing this was all my fault.

"I'm putting everyone in danger. You should just deliver me to my father."

"You are never going back to him. It's best you learn that now." His voice is hard and cruel. I slam my eyes shut as the truth hits me. He's not the man who was there to rescue me.

"You aren't who I thought you were."

"I told you who I was. I told you that I wasn't your savior."

"You killed my brother."

"And soon your father. Revenge will be mine."

"And I'm just a part of it."

His shoulders drop as the words come out of his mouth. "Yes." They hurt more than the physical abuse I received over the years.

My hand comes out before thinking better of it, slapping him across the face. "I hate you."

"Makes two of us. Now, are you ready for the tour?"

"Tour? Have you lost your mind? I don't want to do anything with you again." I shove the damn clothes out of my way as I storm to the bathroom.

"Tough shit, Princess." He slams the door open and

picks me up around the waist, flipping me over his shoulder. I kick him, and then he throws me on the bed, climbing over me with his thigh holding both of my legs firmly so I can't kick again. "Listen, you are testing my patience right now."

"So you're no different than my father, are you?"

"I'm nothing like that bastard. I told you I wouldn't hit you, but maybe you need a good spanking." Roman spins me around, moving faster than I've ever seen him do before. He sits on the edge of the bed with my face down in his lap. He pulls up my blouse and then yanks my pants past my ass. "So sexy. This is what you'll get every time you try shit like you did."

His hand comes down on my right cheek and then my left. Each flat smack of his palm grazed my ass with a sting that I shouldn't like, but I did. He's my kidnapper. Did he plan to kill me like my brother? He goes at it again, and I can't fight the pure arousal. Two more smacks to my bottom, and I'm so turned on I can't figure out which way is up, and now I'm crying.

"Have you had enough?" His fingers dip into my pussy, and it flutters all on its own. "Fuck, you taste good when you're getting your ass ripened." He pushes another finger inside before bringing them back to his mouth.

"You sick animal."

"You haven't seen a taste of the animal I've become." He tosses me on my belly and then yanks my pants down further before dropping to his knees and eating me out from behind. As upset as I am, I can't fight the orgasm ripping through my tight hole. He grabs my juices, and then I feel him stick it one in my ass. It's shocking and yet pleasurable. Still, I fight, pushing back for more. "Don't test me because this cherry hole needs to be filled too. I will own all of you before this is all said and done." He kisses my ass cheeks before pulling up my pants and panties. "By the way, they did a great job on the clothes."

"Who cares?" I pant.

"I do. My wife doesn't wear rags."

"Wife?"

"Yes. That's what I said. Tonight, you will be my wife."

"That's your revenge."

"Call it what you will, but tonight you'll be Katya Semyonova." He kisses my neck and then my lips. "I'll never get enough." Roman adjusts his cock in his slacks which is hard to hide without his suit jacket.

"Are you ready for your tour?"

"I suppose." My body's shaking from the orgasm and the revelation. I don't know what to do, but I'm not going to put up a fight right now.

"That's a much better answer."

He takes his hand in mine and leads me out of the room, locking the bedroom before we go. I don't know how to feel as several men keep their eyes down as we pass them.

"Boss, we have a problem," Alek says, coming up to us. He shuts his mouth and becomes stoic, looking away from me and back to Roman. They begin discussing something in Russian, and Roman continues to get angrier by the second.

"Have you disposed of our last guest?"

"I have."

"Good. We'll have to give him special treatment then. For now, I'm giving my bride a tour of the house. Then I'll finish my business for the day."

"Yes, Boss." He takes my hand and leads me through the foyer. "From here, two staircases lead up to the bedrooms. Down this hall is the kitchen, and then in the other direction is my office. I'll give you a tour of the kitchen to meet the head cook and my housekeeper."

He leads me down the hall, and I see a portrait of a beautiful family with Roman standing beside an older version of himself. He quickly moves past the frame and pushes open the kitchen door. At the stove is a woman about the same age as Olga and another slightly older.

It strikes me that he killed Olga. "He killed Olga," I whisper to myself.

He leans in and says, "She abused you, and that was unacceptable."

"Maria, Angelina, this is my bride, Katya."

"So lovely, like an ice princess."

"If you are hungry, please say something, and they can have it made up."

"Thank you," I tell them, although I refuse to address Roman.

"Excuse us. I have to finish giving my bride the tour."

"I'm not marrying you." I push against his chest.

He grips me close and snarls, "Yes, you are. I don't care if you hate me right now. I will accept nothing less."

Letting go of his harsh grip, he continues his tour. I'm silent as he leads me around, stopping finally in his office. It's beautiful and everything a badass mafia boss would have, which makes sense. Nothing about Roman ever screamed underling.

He sits in his chair behind his desk, dragging me onto his lap. "I have something terrible to do, but first, I need to give you this...."

Unable to look at him, my attention is drawn to the desk, where I see the watch that belonged to my brother. I might not have loved him, but this is cruel. "You stole his watch off his cold body." I jump off his lap, snatch it off the desk, and run. Roman's on me in a second, slamming my body up against the door.

He takes the watch from me and looks at the glass cover. It's cracked. Fury fills his eyes, and he steps back like he's holding it in, and I'm about to feel the abuse he promised I wouldn't.

He steps back and stares into my eyes. There's something missing in his gaze when he says, "You've got what you wanted, Princess. The wedding is off."

Turning his body to make sure he doesn't touch me, Roman yanks the door open and storms out of the room. I'm standing there, looking confused, as several men around quickly step out of his way.

He left the house without another word to me, but he said something to them in Russian.

"Come on, Miss Volchek. Time to go back to your room." Ivan leads me upstairs as several other men leave the house, including Alek. Whatever is going to happen, I hope he's going to be okay.

They open the door, and all the clothes are still in messy piles on the bed and floor. My head is reeling with emotions. To keep them occupied, I fold them and put them back in the bags so they can be taken back. Curling up, I sit in the chair in the corner, refusing food that has been brought up to me several times throughout the day. I've lost my appetite and so much more.

CHAPTER SIX

ROMAN

I CAN'T STAY in the house a moment more before snapping. Getting ahold of Vlad is the only thing that will heal this ache in my chest. Everything wrong in my world is his doing, and nothing can be fixed until he's destroyed.

My head is back in the house and with Katya. I never meant to slam her up against the door like that. I hadn't physically hurt Katya, but I broke my father's watch, and I scared the fuck out of her.

"Where are you going? Have you lost your mind? You're not marrying her anymore?" Alek asks me as he jumps into the passenger seat. It's not smart just for me to run out of the house when I have an enemy eager to do me in. Still, I'm a man of action, and sitting on my hands isn't going to cut it.

"She doesn't want to marry me, and there's no way I'll force her. She's right. You were right. I'm no better than her father, and I've proven that."

"You're not that asshole. If you had seen the look on

her face as you left, it had nothing to do with whatever happened in the room." I hadn't bothered to turn around, too afraid to see what I'd done.

I press my forehead to the steering wheel, knowing I've fully lost my mind and heart. "I can't let her go." The words leave my lips with so much pain.

"I know. You're in love with her, and it's inconvenient that she's his daughter, but she's a treasure, and you know it. Let's get this stress out, handle some business, and go back home so you can start to mend the issues between the two of you."

"Stop being the asshole of reasoning." I turn on the engine, and we speed out of the estate at a rapid speed.

He buckles up with a grin. "A new title. I'll take it, so where are we going?"

"To take off some heads. I'm feeling violent right now, and I have Volchek in my sights. I've had enough of these games."

"We should call in some reinforcements. They're not far behind us." I know they wouldn't just leave me to my own devices, given the current climate.

We go hunting for Volchek's men, but they've scattered like the vermin they are. Abram Petrov's place is my next stop. He's hiding with Volchek, so I want it torn apart, learning everything I can about his involvement with Volchek. We arrive at his rundown hovel in town and find it's already been ransacked. "What the hell? I didn't order this."

"Maybe he has more enemies than you." Pressing the button on the dash, I call Petrov to find out who has it in for his cousin.

"At least it's a reasonable hour," he mutters as he answers the line. "What's up, Roman?"

"Your cousin's place was ransacked. Who else is gunning for the prick?"

"Do you have time for a list? The Crimea Bratva in Omsk is just one to whom he owes money, and there's the Popov Bratva in Moscow, that he pulled a quick one on. He's got his ticket punched, and there's nothing I can do. Fucking bastards have already contacted me looking for payment, but I didn't agree to shit," he scoffs.

"Shit, are they going to come after you?" That's borrowed trouble he doesn't need.

"I hope the fuck not, but these assholes all seem to think that making a deal with him is like making it with me. Hell, I wouldn't make a deal with that idiot."

"Well, watch your back. The Popovs don't play."

"I will. Maybe I'll take a page from Drago's book and find myself an American girl and live there," he chuckles.

"Good luck, my friend." I've found my bride and have no intention of leaving my motherland. I end the call, and we scope out the home, finding everything ruined with the distinct smell of piss and decomposition.

Alek looks at the rubble. "Do you think this is a distraction, or has Abram met with one of his enemies?"

It could be either. However, for now, the answer will have to wait. Abram is the least of my concerns. With so many people after him, there's no need to worry about us getting to him.

"Who knows? Let's go before Volchek's dogs get a whiff of us in the area." If this is a ploy to look like he's run, then someone will be watching to see which of his enemies have stopped by.

"Let's go to Vlad's summer estate." It's only about an hour from where we are, so Alek and I make the drive. We head toward his compound, slowing down as we approach. None of the vehicles are in the vicinity, so we move in closer. I bring out a specialized heat-seeking drone and fly it over the home and scan the area for warm bodies. The property has been abandoned, but from the view it's been rigged with explosives. The bastard was expecting me to come barging in, but I'm not that foolish.

Sergei, one of my operatives who has eyes on Volchek, calls me. "What's going on?"

"He's fled the country. I've intercepted a few calls, but we think he's heading to the States."

"Are you serious?" The fucking pussy.

"Yes. All signs point to him arriving in France and then another flight leaving for New York tomorrow." It could be another ruse or he could just be on the run with his tail between his legs. I've nearly wiped out his entire fortune with a couple of clicks, dismantling his empire from the inside out.

"Also, we still have your guest at the house ready for your questioning."

I think about the conversation I had this morning. "Hello Father Leo. I need a favor."

"Anything for you, my boy."

"I need you to perform a wedding today."

"A wedding today?"

"Yes. Isn't it too soon for a wedding?"

"It's the perfect time." I hear the line click, knowing someone else is listening in. My men run a scan, and it's Volchek's line.

"I suppose I can marry you today if you wish to come to the church."

"No, it will be here, Father Leo."

"This won't make Volchek go away."

"I don't recall asking your opinion on that matter. Get here by four o'clock." I ended the call while my men listen to the

call between Father Leo and Volchek. The words burn in my ears as I learn the truth of my parents' death.

I couldn't believe the information I'd been given this morning regarding his betrayal. I had plans to use him before I made him pay, but I couldn't taint a marriage to my Katya with a murderer pronouncing husband and wife.

"Boss, Boss. You there?" I'd been lost in that fucked up memory and anger from this morning.

"Yes, Sergei. We'll be there shortly." I look to Alek. Time to send the vermin fleeing. Tossing several bombs through the windows, I watch as one of Vlad's two compounds begins to smolder and then explode as the devices inside give way. Enjoying the fun, I sent one more bomb into his fountain that my father recommended to Vlad.

"Where is that asshole at?" Alek asks.

"He's heading to the States."

"I'm betting he's looking for assistance."

"He doesn't know many people in the U.S. that can lend him a hand. He could be there licking his wounds after I nearly bankrupted him this morning. Do you think he'd go to Romanov for help?" They were working on a project together as well as the lies I had whispered about Drago to Vlad.

"That's going to be hard to do, considering Romanov doesn't help anyone and certainly not against you."

"True, but that doesn't mean he wouldn't try. Given that I did say I didn't trust Drago to Vlad's face. If he believes me, then he'll be hoping to find a way inside with one of the most ruthless killers we know."

"Don't worry about it for now. We'll see if that's the

plan after we deal with that little side project at the house," Alek says, driving down the main road.

I'm about to slam his head on the steering wheel. "Don't call her that."

"I was referring to your guest in the cellar." He chuckles hard. "Although it seems she's always on your mind."

"It's like you said." Flipping him off, I take a deep breath and control the rage inside.

"Life is funny like that. Do you want me to take your father's watch in to be fixed?"

"No. I'll do it myself." I don't want anyone else to touch it.

"Okay."

We arrive at the house before midnight, and I go down to the cellar to see my new guest sitting in the chair, and I stare at this rat traitor. "Well, hello, Father Leo." The man is in his mid-forties, a little too clean cut for a priest, something I hadn't noticed before, but it's clear as day now.

"What are you doing? I'm a man of the cloth," he exclaims, trying to free himself from the ropes. "I thought I came here for a wedding."

I nod, tapping my blade against my chin. "Yes, well things change. A man of the cloth? Bullshit."

"You know I've served God for two decades." I roll my eyes because it doesn't mean a thing when you work hand in hand with the devil.

"How long have you been serving Volchek?" He flinches at the question.

"He donates a lot of money to the church that is all." He shakes in his seat as the lies spill from his mouth.

"Blood money. How long?"

"Three years."

"So you sold your soul to the devil for three years and you think being a man of God is supposed to save you from your sins?"

"This isn't in your nature." No, before this, I'd been a hardworking businessman with my hands mostly clean and my conscience clear. All killings I committed were minimal and a part of my growing up in the family. This is completely different.

"No, it's nurture. You and the scum like yourself have nurtured the beast in me while I grieved over my brother." Every nerve in my body vibrates with rage as I press play.

"Leo, I feel like it is time for a repeat performance."

"What Vlad?"

"Go in and take care of the fucker like we did with his family."

"I won't make it out alive. It's not like you're around to go with."

"Fucking coward. It's your fault Piotr found out about our dealings. He had to go and so did that beautiful wife of his. The little twisted version of his father was just extra fun for my boy to enjoy. Now, go there and end him and have my prize brought back to me. She's worth a lot—"

I click the stop button because we've all heard enough. Alek tenses by my side when they mentioned my brother so callously.

"I didn't know he'd kill Ilya." I punched him in the face. Blood drips down his face onto his sacred gowns and my anger triples. Was he dressed like this when he arrived at my parents' home?

We learned that my father been visited by Father Leo with Vlad. He had come there on the pretense of charity work, allowing the devil in to do his deeds. It took a certain level of evil to lead a family to their death knowingly.

"Don't speak his name. You have forgotten your way, father, and unfortunately, there is no redemption for such sins in my eyes." I grab his fingers and twist them, yanking bones until I hear them break. He screams and I don't feel an ounce of guilt for it. Rage only fills my veins.

"I'll do anything to make it up to you." I could strangle him with my bare hands, so I do.

Alek pulls me off him after a moment, making sure I prolong this. I back off as Leo sputters and coughs, trying to breathe.

I pace as I gather myself. "Make it up to me? You helped orchestrate my family's murders and you think that somehow that you could ever make it up to me." I turn to Alek and say, "The gall of this piece of filth."

"I'd say your prayers, father," Alek adds, knowing there's nothing that will save him from my wrath. I don't need any more words or answers. I need his life to end. He does and as soon as he does, I put a bullet in his head.

"No sacred burial for him," I say. Alek nods, and the other men come into the room to handle the cleanup. I send up a silent prayer for my own soul, which has been forever damaged by this.

Unable to see Katya with the blood and sins on my hands, I decide to get to work on destroying the rest of Volchek's properties. With more intel gathered, I return late into the night only to learn that Katya hasn't been interested in eating, according to the last check by Angelina.

Frustrated, I sneak into our bedroom to find her asleep on the chair in our room.

Snagging up some boxers, I jump in the shower to scrub off the grime and blood from the rampage I went on. Once I'm out, dried and dressed, I take all the bags off the bed and put them in the closet to be put away later. Needing to put my princess to bed properly, I scoop my sleeping beauty, pull back the covers, and tuck her under them.

"I'm sorry for everything but loving you." I brush my lips against her temple and then lay there for an hour before my phone vibrates in my pocket. A sinner's work is never done.

CHAPTER
SEVEN

KATYA

I WAKE up in the bed we've shared since I came here, but Roman isn't there and the pillows beside me are cold. Still, I'm not sure how I got into bed. Sitting up, I see all the bags of clothes are gone, so he must have had them removed.

Reeling with sadness, I roll back around in the covers, not wanting to wake up. For the next hour I sluggishly move around the bedroom, feeling broken. Roman's my captor and not the savior I thought he was, and yet, I can't find it in me to hate him. If anything, the feeling is the exact opposite.

The way he made me feel in such a short time has been more intense and real than the entire lifetime I've had in the cottage without a soul who actually cared what happened other than I was still alive at the end of the day. Does that make me a fool? Probably, but I don't care. I want to go back to how it was yesterday before everything went bad.

A knock on the door takes me by surprise. "Come in," I choke out through tears, swiping them away quickly before they can be noticed.

The three girls come in and gasp. "Oh no. We hoped things would be better this morning. Ivan said we were to leave you alone." The trio rushes into the room, closing the door behind them where Ivan stands guard just outside. I catch a frown on his face before the door completely shuts. Great, so everyone knows I'm a wreck. I suppose the cat was out of the bag yesterday, but I've never been around this many people at once, and it's unnerving and comforting at the same time. Still, there's only one person I care to hear from, and he's not coming near me.

"Mr. Semyonov said the clothes should be put away properly," Mariska says, looking at the boxes of shoes next to the closet door.

"They're all going back. I'm not going to be staying here much longer. In fact, I need to find a way out of here," I say, trying to climb off the enormous bed that I'm way too comfortable in.

"Seriously, girl. So, he's pissed about his father's watch. He'll get over it." Anya smacks Anna this time. They have a habit of letting things slip out. What does she mean *his father's watch?*

Anna glares at her sister and says, "Come on. She has to know what's going on by now. I overheard Mr. Semyonov say she knows the truth." I stare at them, completely dumbfounded.

"Know what? He killed my brother, my father's men, and soon my father."

Anya blows a harsh breath before dropping to the bed beside me. Anna sits on the other side and runs her hands through my hair. "I'm sorry, but they all deserve it and *so* much more. They killed Mr. Semyonov's parents and little brother, who was only ten."

"What do you mean?" I gasp, grateful that I'm sitting down because suddenly, the blood feels like it leaves my head.

Mariska comes out of the closet with a hanger in her hand with a look of pain on her face, matching mine. "They were only laid to rest two weeks ago."

"We were there at the service in the back while your father was boldly upfront with your brother. I heard your brother stole the watch off his body after killing Mr. Semyonov's father. It was an anniversary present from his wife."

"So that's why he wants me dead," I mutter.

Anya takes my hand and sits by my legs. "He doesn't want you dead. Maybe he wanted his revenge, but you're so sweet. I bet as soon as he saw you, he couldn't think of hurting you."

Mariska adds, "But he's hurting pretty bad. We all know we'd be devastated if it was one of us. Still, if he's not careful, he could lose everything."

"What do you mean?" The thought of something terrible happening to Roman sends pain straight to my chest like nothing else.

"Your father won't be satisfied with anything less than Mr. Semyonov's death. Along with taking control of all Mr. Semyonov's businesses, of course. He didn't mind killing a little kid, so going after another grown man won't mean a thing to him."

Suddenly I remember the picture that we passed on the way to the kitchen yesterday had been Roman's family and my family had taken that away from him.

"Wow." I don't know what else to say as a pawn in a war that my father started, and that Roman wants to end.

"Don't start crying again, Katya. Please don't. It's crazy complicated, but it will get better." Anna hugs me first, then the other two girls throw their arms around me right after.

"How about we do some girly things and eat some food? I'm sure you're starving by now."

"I am kind of hungry."

"Good. I'll tell my brother."

"While we wait, let's get these clothes put away. I can't stand to see a good fabric wrinkled," Mariska bemoans. I giggle and feel a little less miserable.

Ten minutes later an entire tray of food is brought up. It's large enough to serve a dozen people, and when I tell Angelina that she just smiles and says, "It's good to see you eat."

I take a fresh strawberry and dip it in some crème. "So what do you girls do for fun? You're the first women I've actually met that weren't mean to me."

"Well, we need to teach you how to fight for one. Although, I doubt Roman would like you getting your pretty face scuffed up."

"We're sisters so we spend a lot of time watching movies, going to the malls, gossiping."

"Your mom is staying here as well?" I don't know what it's like to have a proper family, sisters or a mother. It must be wonderful even when they're bickering and slapping each other for something.

"Yes, but she's napping right now. She has a nasty cold, so she's been eating a special broth that Maria made her." I pluck at a few grapes and eat them.

"You're eating only the fruit. You're missing all the

good stuff." Anya passes me a crème filled dessert, and it looks incredible. The second it hits my tongue I know I'm going to put on twenty pounds hanging out with the girls. A moan escapes my lips and I take a second bite right away.

"See, living here is not so bad," Anna says. My mind goes straight to Roman and how he must hate me. None of these excesses could make up for the loss of his affection. Was it all an act or, like the girls say, he truly wants me? I know he lusts after me because even when he was angry, he gave me an intense orgasm and wanted to marry me, but is his hatred for my birth father greater than his interest in me?

"Uh oh. You sent her off the deep end again."

"Sorry." Anya squeezes me.

"I need to be alone," I whisper.

"Call us when you want to hang out." I nod and sit in bed, thinking about Roman for the thousandth time today.

CHAPTER
EIGHT

ROMAN

I'VE HAD ALL I can take of staying away from Katya. It's been almost a full twenty-four hours since I've spoken to her and the last words that we shared weren't kind ones. Two steps at a time, I fly up the stairs to my bedroom. I reach for the knob just as Ivan's sisters open it. Seeing them, I step back and let them exit and close the door. "What's going on?" I asked in a hushed voice.

The dark-haired one says, "We just wanted to comfort her."

"Did it work?" I want to know how bad it is before going in and that probably makes me a coward, but I've never been in this position before.

One of the blondes answers, "We don't know. We thought so, but she has a lot going on in that head of hers."

I nod and enter the room, locking it behind me.

When I turn to look at her, her head is ducked down, shoulders slumped, sitting in the middle of our bed. The sadness drives me into action.

"Aurora, look at me," I commanded.

She raises her head, and there's an air of attitude mixed in with those sad blue eyes. "Have you forgotten my name already?"

Shaking my head, I rush closer to the bed. "No, but you answered."

"I'm sorry, Roman." I'm taken aback by her apology and freeze on the spot. "I'm really sorry." She pouts, and it's the fucking cutest thing, but I'm not sure if I'm being played or she's actually serious. I kick off my shoes and climb on the bed.

Cupping her chin, I stare into her eyes. "I already told you... you're not leaving, so you don't need to coax your way out of getting away from me because it's not happening."

She pulls away from me and stands up. "No, I don't want to leave. It's wrong and right all at the same time." She starts pacing around, biting that bottom lip of hers while her long pale blonde hair blows with the gentle breeze she's creating. I reach out and snag her hand, stopping her movements.

"What is it?" I have to touch her to feel sane again.

The tears in her eyes are breaking me. "I'm sorry about what he did to your family. I wish that I could make it better, take it back or even replace them with my life. I can't imagine the pain you're going through right now." I'm killing off her family and she feels sorry for me. "I get that it sounds crazy, but even though you went there to harm me, you became my savior."

I can't hear Katya talk about my previous thoughts, so I pull her to my chest, silencing the dark past. "I was never going to kill you." It's the truth even if I tried to act tough.

From the start I had nothing against her, but the fact of the matter was I couldn't let Vlad have anything left.

She lifts her head to look at me. "But you were going to hurt me."

Shaking my head, I disagree. "I didn't know what to do with you even before I saw you. Alek was right. Above all, you were just as innocent as my brother, and I had no right to come after you."

She smiles and then frowns. "I'm glad you did. They were going to sell me."

"I overheard Olga's comments to you that night. You couldn't imagine the anger I felt for a complete stranger. It shocked me."

Katya presses her hand over my chest. "He never loved me; he let Olga beat me. I tried to tell him, hoping it would stop, but he said I deserved it. I needed to learn how to behave like a dutiful wife."

"So, he planned on marrying you off to someone?" Rage consumes me at the thought of her belonging to anyone else when she was always meant to be mine. I'm tempted to hunt down anyone who even knew of her existence and end them just in case they wanted her for themselves.

"I can only assume so. Why keep me alive all these years if he wanted nothing to do with me? You came in and gave me a taste of what the real world was like. Even if you don't want to marry me anymore and want to send me away, I'll have had a taste of what happiness can be."

Gripping her tightly, I press my hardened length against her mound. "I told you I'm never letting you go, so you can get that shitty idea out of your head. We'll get married when you are ready, my Princess."

"What about my father?" Just the mention of him turns my veins to ice.

Looking into her eyes, I give her the honesty I'd held back since we met. "I'm going to have to kill him."

"He's not going to give up until he kills you." Her genuine fear for my safety is sweet and heartwarming, and it gives me hope that after all is said and done she won't despise me for what I have to do.

"He's a trapped rat, but I won't let him take me out. Now kiss me before I lose my mind." She throws her arms around me, and I feel whole again the second her lips touch mine.

"I need your kisses. I'm sorry I broke the watch."

"You didn't break it. I did, but I still shouldn't have practically tackled you."

"I thought it was kind of nice." Her brows rise and fall as she tries flirting with me and it's working.

"Katya, you surprise me every chance you get."

"Well, I'm learning new things every day." She winks at me, and I can't resist kissing her again. The way she feels in my arms is incredible.

She gently pulls away and looks up at me nervously. "Is my father still out there?"

"I don't know where he fled to in the U.S., but he's gone running."

"Does that mean we're safe for now?" The brightness in her eyes sends my cold heart soaring for this beauty.

"You'll always be safe with me."

She kisses me, and then I lose it, carrying her over to the bed. "It's time to make up for lost time."

"I need you, Roman. Love me."

"Forever." Slowly, I strip her clothes down, taking care

to kiss every inch of her body until I have her worked up. Then my hips slide between hers, and my cock pushes its way into her tight hole, claiming her in gentle, blissful passion.

Her body moves with mine, rocking with every roll of my hips. "I need you to tell me you're staying forever, Katya, my Princess."

"I never want to leave you, Roman."

"Good, because I want to keep you forever." Our mouths brush together messily as I move up and down from her chin to her lips. I can't get enough of our languid lovemaking. Her walls flex around me in a steady rhythm as she comes, and I fall over, spilling my seed inside her. I send up a silent prayer that we made one of many sons today.

As we both come down, I realize there's a tray of fruit beside us, and I bring a strawberry to her pretty lips. "I need to feed you and our babies."

She bites it without hesitation or argument. "I love strawberries."

I kiss her lips and groan. "I love them too."

We lay in bed for the rest of the day, letting all the troubles stay where they were. No more talk about her father as I put on movie after movie. Alek keeps me in the loop to reassure me that the house is safe and secure and Volchek is still abroad.

Every giggle from her lips makes the world right around me. I could almost forget about everything else.

THE SUN IS OUT, BUT THE TEMPS HAVE DROPPED, AND MY POOR Katya looks chilly as she sits on our bedroom balcony, drinking her coffee. "You don't have to be out here. I had no idea the temps would have fallen so fast." I bring out a robe and drape it around her slender shoulders.

She tilts her head up at me with her nose turning pink from the cold. "It's actually nice. It's just been a long time since I've been outside that I'm a little nervous."

"You don't have anything to worry about here. Although, I need you to come in now because I've got matters to attend to, and I want to ensure your safety. Let's go up to our room for now." Yesterday had been an enjoyable break, but unfortunately, we can't have peace until I get rid of her father. She doesn't challenge me, which is good. The girls stay at Ivan's wing of the estate so that he can keep an eye on them and his mother, who is slowly improving from a cold.

Just then, my phone rings. It's Sergei. "What's going on?"

"Volchek's calling on Drago Romanov. According to our source, he thinks you two have issues and is hoping to bribe him."

"Are you serious?" I had a feeling he'd try Drago as a last resort.

"Yes. We have a string of texts between Vlad and Abram." So, the fucker isn't dead yet. I got a bullet for him when he does appear, or maybe I'll save him for the Popov family as a peace offering. "They're headed to Chicago, although from the texts, it doesn't look like Drago has any idea they're coming."

"Send them to me," I command.

"They are already headed your way." My phone goes off to a string of texts, showing Vlad getting nervous and looking for allies, but he has none, so he's taking a last shot at Drago for help.

"Thank you for these."

"Do you think Romanov would assist him?" Alek asks again. We both know it wouldn't happen, but how can we work it out to our benefit? If Drago feels insulted or threatened, he'll kill Vlad before he leaves Romanov's estate.

"Not for all the money in the world. Drago has morals even if he's an icy prick."

"What do you want us to do?"

"Let Vlad come for me." Katya gasps as I end the call. I'd forgotten that she was standing there. Cupping her face, I kiss her lips. "Relax, my sweet little princess. He can't get to me, and I'm ready to drop him in a heartbeat. Besides, he's fled the country, so I have some time to prepare even more than I already have. Right now, I have to speak with my men. I'm sorry."

She clings to my sleeve. "Please be careful."

"Absolutely. I have a lot to lose." I kiss her once more before leaving my bedroom.

"Don't let anyone in. Anyone." I look at my guard and give him a warning that I'm deathly serious. As much as I like Ivan's sisters, I have to trust that she doesn't have any enemies on the inside.

I head down to my office, close the door, and call my friend in Chicago. Shit, I forget to check the time over there, but when I look, it's around the early morning hours. Hopefully, I catch him. Drago manages to pick up on the second ring.

"Hello, Brat," he greeted me.

"He's coming to you. I've taken her, and I will have my revenge." Drago and I are quite similar now more than ever. I'd never been this dark or violent, while he's always been cold and deadly. Still, I'm not letting anyone come between Katya and me.

"Oh, yes?" He's the one who helped me find the little ice princess in her forest prison. His help was instrumental in locating her so quickly, and I'll forever be grateful to him because if I hadn't found her when I did, she could have been moved or sold to some asshole.

"He wants your aid in destroying me." I can't hide the rage that comes out with every word.

"He will never acquire it," Drago snarls on the other end. I never once doubted my friend, no matter what I made everyone else believe. His character, although dark and cold, has always been trustworthy.

"Yes, yes. I know, but he is desperate and on the run. I've taken everything but the last vestiges of his power that he clings to. He will give you *her* if you kill me. I won't let anyone have her."

"You know where I stand." I do, which means he will have to make a decision, and I want it to benefit me.

"Then what will you do when he comes? I want his head, Drago."

"I shall deliver it if you like," he answers with a smile in his voice. It would be just like Drago to bring me Vlad's head impaled on a spike for a gift.

"No, I want to take it first." If anyone is going to destroy the bastard, it will be me.

"Good, I will make the deal and journey with him to you. Da?"

"Sounds perfect. Thank you, my brother."

I share with him my plan for his arrival, assuming that Vlad will actually follow through on the supposed texts that I received. We end the call, telling me he has to get back to his little morsel. That is something we have in common. Still, I have matters to discuss with my men before I can head up and see my woman and let her know all is well for now.

CHAPTER
NINE

KATYA

MORNING COMES, and it's a repeat of the other day with my pussy being completely destroyed by Roman's fabulous tongue. I don't need to speak Russian to know he's enjoying it with every dirty word slipping past his lips. The feeling is indescribable as he drives me wild.

Roman makes me come once more before coming up for air. Then with his enormous cock, he slides deep inside me in one fluid motion. Working in and out of me, he takes us both over the edge again, and my body trembles with all the sensations.

We crumple onto the bed and roll around as he continues to kiss all over my neck and face. "You feel so damn good, my little princess," he whispers in my ear, pulling me in close.

I turn around in his arms and ask, "Why do you call me that?" I assume it has to do with the whole Sleeping Beauty thing.

He brushes my sweaty hair away from my face and

gazes into my eyes. "Because, sweetheart, I've been known as the bratva prince. Therefore, you must be my princess." He's called me his princess from the moment we met. My heart does flips with the fairytale I'm living. It will come crashing down on me at any moment, but I hope it doesn't.

"I've got something for you." He sits up and then goes into the drawer next to the bed.

"Really? Like you haven't given me everything already."

"You deserve so much more than I could ever give you, Katya."

He hands me a pretty square box larger than my hand but not taller than an inch. I open it to find a phone like his. "What? A phone?"

"Yes. I know you had that old thing. This is a new model, and it will take a while to learn how to use it." I can't believe he gave me a phone. That's an insane amount of trust.

"Does it only have your number?" It's the only thing my father had on my old one.

"Well, not only mine, but it's the first number I put in there. You have Alek, Ivan's, the girls' numbers, and Angelina's."

"I can't believe it." I stare at it in amazement. "But what do I need it for if I can't leave?"

"You will be able to go out sometimes. Besides, the girls won't be staying with us long."

"Are you serious?"

"Extremely serious. Actually, there's something else important about this phone. I had Alek set it up with some special features, although it forced him to add additional space to the phone." He taps the phone a couple of times, and then up comes a list of music.

"There are over two thousand songs in English on here. Most of them are older, like The Beatles you mentioned." I let it slip while we were watching movies when a song came on that I loved.

I throw my arms around him and tackle him to the bed. "I'm sorry."

"Baby girl, don't ever be sorry for throwing your sexy, naked body on me." He growls and pins me to the bed pressing play on the music button on the phone.

We made love again, and I know today can't get any better. An hour later, we come up for air, and breakfast is brought to us. "I need to get ready, but you can take your time," he says, snatching a piece of toast off the tray.

I spend the morning dancing around as I shower and prepare for the day. Tonight, I'm going to make Roman my soup to thank him for being so sweet. Maria and Angelina have been smiling at me because they think I've lost it. "You are so happy, and we absolutely love it. Soon this house will be filled with laughter and babies."

It reminds me that maybe his family had lived here before. "Did his family live here before they died?" Other than a picture or two, I didn't see anything that looked like anyone else lived here. Even though I know they were killed, I don't know the details, and I don't want to, either.

Maria shakes her head. "No, this is Roman's home. They had their home not too far away."

"Wow, it smells good in here," Alek says, coming into the kitchen and rubbing his stomach. Roman follows, growling at him.

I smile at Alek, earning me a growl from Roman.

"Thank you. I'm cooking, and the soup should be done in about an hour."

"Alek, stop it, or I'm not cooking for you anymore." Maria rolls her eyes at him

"Maria, don't be getting jealous now. Roman's not going to let her cook for me all the time. You'll always be my girl." He winks at her. It's so funny that Roman is acting jealous of Alek over nothing because there's no need for it.

"Anyone that cooks for you makes you a happy man," she says, swatting his hand as he reaches for the fresh bread she's slicing.

"She's not wrong," Roman says, sliding around the counter to pull me in his arms. "I hope you're not overdoing it in here."

"I'm not. I love cooking, and it's nice to use new and pretty toys to do it."

"Anything you want, just tell me." He kisses my neck and then pulls away to snatch a slice of bread.

"Slick," Alek mutters.

"Nice moves, Mr. Semyonov."

"I got more moves for you." He puts the slice of bread to my lips, and I bite. An involuntary moan escapes. "Fuck, woman. None of that in public."

"Now, I'm really getting jealous. That must be some damn excellent bread."

"Oh, shut up and have one," Maria says, stuffing one in his hand. He smiles cheekily, and then their phones go off simultaneously.

Roman and Alek start speaking fast in Russian, and then Maria takes my hand, tugging me from the room. "Roman," I call out.

He rushes to my side and kisses me hard before pulling away. "I love you," he says as he leaves me with Maria.

We hurry to the middle of the living room where the girls and their mother meet us, Angelina and Ivan following behind. He hits a switch, enters a code, and the floor opens. "Inside now," Ivan barks. Maria goes in first down the stairs with me right behind her. All the women enter, and then Ivan closes the door, trapping us inside.

"Oh my God. What's going on? Where are we?"

"We're in the safe room of the house. We'll be protected here from all danger, including full-on bomb blasts, so try to calm down." Oh yeah, that's just going to calm me right down. A bomb blast while Roman's out there and could be killed.

I throw my hands up in the air, ready to rip my hair out. "Calm down? Roman's out there."

"We know. Your father's here."

I slam my hands down on the desk near the entrance. "Can we stop calling him that now? He's never been a father to me."

"Of course. Volchek has arrived with a fleet of men ready for battle."

This day went from wonderful to the worst day of my life in a heartbeat. One moment I'm rolling around in Roman's arms, and the next, we're in panic mode. I've been sent off to a room in the house away from him, hiding with the rest of the women. I look at all the control panels as they light up with the cameras from outside. We can see the action from where we are.

Ivan's mother and sisters decide to stay clear of that area, but I can't look away.

I start pacing back and forth. After a minute of losing

my mind, I need to get out of here and find Roman. Searching for the open sesame button on the door, Mariska grabs my arm and stops me. "Don't even think about going out there, Katya. Roman would lose his mind. He has to protect you; he can't do that if you go out there and distract him." She's right, and yet it doesn't make it any better.

"Did you see that big guy that came with my father?"

"Yes, that's Drago Romanov. Don't worry about him. He's not on your father's side," Maria says, patting my hands. I cling to her and turn away from the cameras because that man screams dangerous, and if he betrays Roman, I can't watch it and be able to do nothing.

CHAPTER TEN

ROMAN

THE THING about rats is that they're willing to sneak in and attack any way they can. Sergei reported that Vlad and a handful of men arrived at the airport over an hour ago. Drago and his main guy were with him, which I already knew since I'd been in communication with my friend since I learned about Vlad's plan.

With my last contact, Drago informed me that they'd separate themselves from Vlad's men the second they arrived at my estate and to be prepared.

I came in to check on my princess in the kitchen and see her before I had to send her away. I knew any minute the alarm would sound, but I selfishly stole a few more moments with her, needing to breathe her in and feel her as if it would be my last time.

The first alarm sounds in the distance. They're five miles out, so I send the women to the panic room where they'll be safe. My priority is protecting Katya while getting the evil out of our lives. I hadn't meant to say those words so carelessly when she deserved to hear them said properly, but I meant them with all of my heart.

Men prepare their weapons as the seven carloads of men appear out of the line of trees. Drago sent me a message that they were coming with about forty men from Vlad's allies he corralled at the airport. I'm sure with all the same promise of Katya and his empire, which I have decimated. That's a lot more than I expected, but my thirty men can handle them.

The first vehicle rams my iron gate, but I already removed the hinges, so it easily falls. Vladimir's face is shocked and then he gives the order. His men still come blazing through my driveway, shooting with pretty heavy firepower.

Drago and his man pop out of the third vehicle and roll to the side, ducking past the fountain and moving behind a large tree. Before his men can see it coming, Drago opens fire on the last vehicle, sending it careening into a tree on the lawn. His buddy tosses a quick explosive at the car in front of it, sending that car up in flames. Several bodies fall out of the burning car, trying to shoot as they burn.

"Traitor," Vlad calls out from his position, tucked safely in his armored vehicle like a coward. His men now split the gunfire between the two areas, giving us a reprieve. My eyes are solely focused on Vladimir, who is in the second car, hiding while everyone else does the work for him. Three guys come barreling forward with rapid-firing machine guns. From the roof, Ivan sends out a grenade, landing on the fuckers and sending them all over the lawn.

The first vehicle plows through the dead bodies, charging my men, who continue firing. We set out two dozen spike strips in the driveway and grass. We watched as all the vehicles began popping tires and coming to a full stop, forcing them to jump out only to meet my guys hanging out in a tree. Two of the vehicles slammed into each other with momentum, creating a wall of SUVs. Still, my men get to work.

Bodies litter the ground as Drago and his man maneuver around them, running alongside Alek and me. "I want Volchek," I shout for all to hear. "No one but me kills him." I want Volchek to hear that shit as well. The need to destroy him has only grown.

"Yes, Boss," Alek says.

Drago nods and gives me a warning. "Careful. He's a trapped animal."

I nod.

"Anyone who kills this bastard gets to enjoy my daughter's pussy," Volchek sounds off from a megaphone in his vehicle. That's it. I lose my cool.

"I'm going to kill that son of a bitch," I roar. "It ends today."

"Fuck," I hear Drago snarl, but that's all I hear because my ears are ringing with rage.

I run toward the SUV with Vladimir Volchek hiding like the bitch he is. As I move closer, two more guys come running my way, and Drago and Alek take them out.

Six or more come from the next vehicle, and they start spraying, shooting at any target in their path, but I'm so focused on getting to Vlad that I don't see if my men have gotten them all. I'm almost to Vlad when I feel the burn of a bullet to my chest. Then out of nowhere I'm hit with something heavy.

"You idiot," Drago snarls.

"Roman," I hear Katya's voice in my head as I fall to the ground; everything goes cold and dark. I failed.

"Roman, please open your eyes." The sound of an angel stirs me. I wake up in my bed with Katya fawning all over me. *I must have woken up in heaven.* "You're alive," she says, sobbing beside me. Her pale blonde hair falls around her face, creating a halo and her icy blues are bright.

What the hell happened? I think, trying to look around the room. The sun is lightly peeking through the curtains, but my eyes are still a little unfocused.

"I am?" I ask, groaning in pain.

"Yes, but it was pretty close," Katya says, pressing kisses on my face. I bring her close, kissing her hard until I feel her yelp. Quickly, I release her and allow my eyes to adjust to the light.

"I'm sorry." She rubs her cheek. I see the red mark on her face, so I rub my face and feel the day-old scruff.

"Next time, cool your heels," Drago calls from the doorway without a shirt on and his waist bandaged. I want to snap about not wearing clothes in front of my woman, but I'm guessing he's the reason I'm still kicking, and I owe him a lot. His man hands him a dress shirt that he gingerly puts on.

"Did you get him?" I ask.

He scoffs. "No thanks to your ass."

I close my eyes and feel the shame of letting myself get carried away by emotions, and Volchek almost won. "I lost it. He was goading me."

"You fell for his shit. We blocked his exits, and you ran right in his path. Hot-headed as hell, like we couldn't have taken all those other pussies out easily, which we did." He shakes his head and holds onto the doorframe.

"Then what happened to you there?" I ask, pointing to his bandaged waist.

"That was courtesy of your rat problem."

"Rat problem?"

"As soon as you're feeling up to it, there's a nice fat rat in your cellar that needs exterminating."

"What?"

"I could have just blown his brains out, but I know you wanted that honor. After all, you were willing to die just to get at him. I promised I'd save him for you. Consider it a wedding present."

He winks and then stumbles back out of the room with the help of Ivan and his man.

Alek comes into the room, looking unscathed. "Roman, you gave us a damn good scare."

"How long have I been out?" I ask.

He pours me a glass of water. "Here. Almost two whole days. Surprisingly we didn't lose any men. A couple of wounded soldiers, but everyone will make it."

"What happened to Abram?"

"He never made it out of America. Drago said that Volchek sold him to Popov for some soldiers. Although they're not pleased to know they ended up dead. It wasn't supposed to be a war between us."

"Fuck, are we going to have another problem?"

"Nah, the opposite, in fact. They're hoping to create some truce. They don't want trouble for any of their family members right now. The men that took that assignment had a choice, and they made it. Still, he wants to talk to you when you've recovered."

"Okay. Good to know. Now, when can I move?" I grumble, wanting to get back to business and start living my life without Volchek in the shadows.

"The doctor will be here in twenty minutes and then you can be evaluated." I roll my damn eyes and hate that my enemy is tied up in the cellar and there's nothing I can do about it until I recover.

"Okay. Alek, do me a favor. Since I can't just dispose of our guest, make him comfortable." I wink, knowing that Alek will keep him souping until I'm ready to handle the matter personally.

"Already on it. Gave him the luxury suite with the rustic look." He grins. Perhaps my long recovery might be worth it after all. Daily torture or the thought of torture will drive him mad.

"Perfect."

"What about the cleanup?" I don't want Katya to see any of the mess or the authorities asking too many questions.

"It's already done. The team went to work quickly. Get some rest until the doctor comes. You look like shit."

"You're lucky I'm stuck in this bed."

"I know. I'm taking advantage of it. I've eaten most of the soup Katya made."

"What?" I growl.

"I didn't want it to go bad. It was delicious." I grab my pillow and toss it toward him and he runs from the room.

Katya's beautiful giggle from beside me draws my attention back to her. "It's good to see you two together. He's a really good friend."

"He ate my soup. How good of a friend is he?" I say, feeling cheated out of her cooking.

"To be fair it wasn't that good. We all forgot about it and it became more of a stew." I suppose they were definitely busy.

"Fine. Enough about food. I want something else to taste."

"Behave, Roman. You almost died."

"I know. It's all the more reason for me to want to hold you close and feel you in my soul." Even though every ounce of movement causes pain, I can't resist running my hands up and down her body. With a grunt, I flip her onto me and rub her pussy on my cock.

"Roman," she protests, trying to stop me, but I hold her tightly and roll her hips on me. Her protests turn to whimpers.

A knock at the open doorway sends Katya from my arms. "Maybe you'll listen to the doctor," she huffs.

"Probably not," the doctor mutters, coming into the room.

"He's a smart man."

It took a week to get stronger because apparently trying to fuck Katya all the time isn't a wise idea when there's still a decent wound to my chest. "Are you ready to get this over with?" Alek asks as we leave my office.

"More than ever."

"I'm here for whatever you need." He grips my shoulder and squeezes.

"I know. I owe you."

"No you don't. I did this not only for you, but for Ilya, and I'd do it all over again, my friend." I pull my friend in for a hug and then we get our act together because there's hell to pay. It's after midnight when we head down to the cellar, waiting for the moment that's been long overdue.

In a chair, weak and soiled is the man who destroyed my family.

"Roman," he croaks, doing his best to look completely pathetic and helpless which means nothing to me.

"Don't bother pleading for your life. It won't save you."

"I'm not. If it wasn't for that traitor, I would have had you. You're weak and there will be others to come after you when I'm gone." What in the world made him think Drago would choose him over me?

"I don't think so. You need to learn that money can't buy everything. It didn't help your sorry ass. Now you're going to die, and I get to keep the best part."

"All of this is over that stupid little bitch." I try not to let him goad me again. When he doesn't get the reaction out of me, he continues. "I should have dumped her in an orphanage or slit her throat the second I killed her mother."

"And yet you didn't. Did you think she was more profitable when she grew up?"

"It wasn't just the money. She wasn't my kid and my wife paid with her life. I've enjoyed knowing that her biological father suffered for all these years, and I planned on selling her to his crew, eventually. Your father ruined it."

"Selling her to whom?" I'm fucking tired of these guessing games. Every single one of these assholes want to play like it's going to save them. If anything it drives me crazy and I take it out on them.

"None of your business. He'll forever suffer not knowing what happened to his little baby girl, and that makes me fucking happy. I should have torn into that little bitch. She did after all look like a blonde version of her mother who wasn't bad on the eyes."

I need to breathe and remember he can't goad me into reacting. Everything done today will be deliberate and not instigated by his words. "Enough of the talking. You killed my family to keep your revenge all these years and for nothing because I've made Katya mine forever."

Alek brings the salt over, holding it with pride and I grin. "You may not want to speak and that's fine because I only care about your screams." One by one I make cuts on the old bastard's hands, his scalp, and then his feet.

"Alek, you can do the honors." I point to the salt.

"Thank you, Roman." He walks up to a frightened Vlad and pours. Vlad screams and squirms with every granule, but Alek just pours a bit more. Once he's emptied the entire container, we stand back and watch. It gets rather boring pretty quickly. I'd rather be upstairs with my beloved princess, holding her and celebrating our future.

"I'm over this, Alek," I say. Pulling out my gun, I shoot Vlad in the head.

"Good. We'll clean this up." When I leave the room, I feel a weight lifted off my shoulders. It's over and my family has been avenged.

The moment I reached my bedroom, I looked over to our bed and saw Katya sleeping, so I go take a shower. Scrubbing myself clean, I don't hear my little princess until her feet patter into the bathroom and she opens the glass shower door. She presses her naked body to my back. "I love you, Roman."

"It's over. It's over."

"I know." She grabs the loofa from me and starts washing my body. Slowly she reaches my cock and strokes it, losing the sponge. The water beads off my body as my woman moves around in front of me before dropping to her knees.

I can't take my eyes off the sight before me. Her bright blues look up as she grips my shaft, squeezing and stroking it. Then her soft, pink lips wrap around the tip and I'm done for. She slowly takes me down inch by inch, sucking on my cock with such love. I stare down, watching how gorgeous she looks on her knees, pleasing me.

"Katya, I'm going to come."

She pops her lips off my cock and looks up. "Then come for me. This is just for you." She slides her tongue along the thick vein under my shaft and then up to the tip, slipping me back into her warm mouth. Her cheeks hollow out as she works me down, blowing me until I'm about to unload. I can't take it any longer and grip her hair, holding her still as I take over and fuck her pretty, little throat. My hot load shoots quickly, my vision goes black for a second, and I fall back, leaning against the shower wall as I try to catch my breath.

When I look at Katya, she's smiling proudly on her knees, naked and sexy. I just came and I could go again just from the sight before me.

As she goes to stand, I help her up and hold her close. "Thank you."

"You're welcome," she says with a bit of sass.

CHAPTER
ELEVEN

KATYA

THE BACK of the estate has been redone and decorated for our special day. It's a winter wonderland around us except for where all the guests are set up. As mounds of fresh snow lie around us, the ground beneath my feet is covered in fake grass that looks so natural.

A long white path filled with flowers leads to us where we stand in front of the officiant. With our hands, united Roman says his vows to me. Three weeks ago, I was afraid I wouldn't have gotten this chance. Thankfully, he pulled through and is as stubborn as ever.

Everyone is dressed in fur wraps or elegant coats while the industrial heater keeps the gazebo reasonably warm. I have on a beautiful white and blue winter cape, draped over my shoulders and I feel like an ice princess, but no one looks better than the man in front of me.

Like the day I met him, he stands tall in all black, dark hair damp from the fallen snow. Except he has a large black and gray fur-lined cloak that makes him look like a warrior. If there wasn't a crowd of people, I'd pounce on him right now.

The ceremony ends and Roman leads us through the throng of people. There's someone new in the crowd of onlookers who I don't recognize even though something about him is strangely familiar. I can't place him.

Given that I've met no one outside of the estate and my father's men, I wonder if he's trouble. Although looking at his face, I can't seem to get a negative feeling from him.

Cameras go off as they get photos of us. Mariska, Anna, and Anya have been a tremendous help in getting this done. Anna and Anya were my bridesmaids while Mariska was acting as the official wedding planner slash mother hen.

If I didn't know better, I would think Mariska was thirty, not twenty. Without her this wouldn't have been the gorgeous ceremony. She even picked out Roman's cloak which I have to give her a gift for because I plan to be wrapped up only in that tonight while my husband devours me.

Roman raises his hands and the crowd silences. "Please proceed to the ballroom for the reception. I need a moment alone with my bride." He takes me back to his office where the man who caught my attention earlier is waiting for us.

"Katya, I wanted you to meet someone who has been looking for you for a long time. This is Aleksandr Sidorov, your true father." My eyes widen and I see the same blues that I see in the mirror every day.

"Hello, my darling little princess. I thought I'd only see you when I finally passed on."

"I don't understand."

"I don't know the details all the way, my love, but before he died, Vlad said you weren't his, and the father needed to suffer. I didn't know what he meant, but I kept trying to find answers until our wedding announcement was made. He contacted me and as a guest already invited, I knew the second he arrived that you were his daughter."

"My little flower, your mother had been Vladimir Volchek's wife. We met when she ran away from him. I didn't know it and we made you. He found her and she returned to him with you still growing inside her. Right before you were born, she came running back to me, and I took care of you both."

Tears fill my eyes as I listen. Roman holds me close and I lean on him for support.

"When you were two months old, your mother ran again with you or so I believed. She had been killed, and you were gone."

I gasp. "Forgive me if this is too much," he says.

"No, please tell me."

"Volchek swore he had nothing to do with her death or disappearance. We could never find any proof that he did. At the time, I hadn't had the power I do now, and he knew it. My family believed you were sent to an orphanage, or he had killed you as well. For years, I hoped you would show up. I've searched so many orphanages throughout Russia and Ukraine but never found a trace."

"That's why he kept me hidden in a forest. He said I'd been almost kidnapped as a baby, and he didn't want anyone to try again."

"I wish he was still alive so I could kill him." My birth father's eyes darken with rage and pain. Standing up, I go over and give him a hug. "Princess." He clings to me tightly as his voice cracks.

"I'm sorry for not finding you sooner." He looks over to Roman and says, "I'm sorry about your father. I believe he had uncovered the truth. The day he died I'd received a message that he wanted to meet with me."

"When I was a boy, my father learned that Vlad had a daughter, but he didn't know the truth either or he would have said something. As far as we were ever told, his wife and child died in childbirth."

"He enjoyed his torture."

Roman pulls me to his side. "Yes, and now he's gone. So let us celebrate this reunion."

"First, my darling girl. I want you to have this." He pulls out a small photo and gives it to me. "I've had this for nineteen years." It's a picture of my mother smiling with him as he holds me in his arms.

"Oh my goodness." I cry again as a world of emotions hits me. "It's beautiful."

"I didn't mean to make you cry."

"I'm just so happy." I cling to Roman who stares at the photo in awe. I truly look like a mix of both of them. I have his eyes and hair, the rest of my mother's features.

Although, I take a closer look at the picture, and there's something off about her expression. It doesn't look happy like I thought. It reminds me of the times Olga got away with hitting me and she was gloating. Maybe it's just the photo, and I'm making too much out of it.

"I know this is asking a lot, but I hope I can stay in your life, Katya."

I look to Roman, knowing how delicate these wars and alliances can be and hope he says yes. "Don't look to me, my beautiful wife. Whatever makes you happy will please me."

Smiling, I kiss his cheek and then throw my arms around my real father who wholeheartedly welcomes the embrace.

"After all, our children will need at least one grandparent."

"Are you?" my father asks.

"Am I what?" I ask, looking at him confused.

"You must forgive her. She did, after all, live in a cottage with little to no human interaction." I swat him and he says, "I'm teasing, but he's asking if you're already pregnant."

I blush, knowing the answer, and both sets of eyes are staring at me in awe.

"Yes. I found out this morning." Roman whisks me up in the air, twirling me around.

"I'm going to be a grandfather." He falls back in the chair behind him and places his hand over his mouth.

"Do you not have any other children?" I questioned. It would be nice to have siblings like the girls have.

His shoulders slump "No. When you were taken, I was too afraid to start a new family and lose a child. Instead, I built the empire with a fire no one could put out, and I ruled over it while my brothers had children."

"Well, there are a lot of eligible ladies out there," I say.

"I'm too old for them."

A knock at the door interrupts our conversation. "Come in."

"Katya, I hope you haven't ruined your dress. We still have to take pictures," Mariska storms into the office and halts as my father stands tall.

"Mariska, I'd like you to meet my real father, Aleksandr Sidorov." Her mouth hasn't closed yet.

"Too old… hmmm…" I muttered to Roman.

"Hello, dark enchantress." I think my father still has it.

"We're just going to greet our guests and get ready for pictures. Can you show my father around please?"

She only nods, unable to speak, eyes dazed.

CHAPTER
TWELVE

ROMAN

LITTLE BY LITTLE, life returns to a calm, peaceful living. Although Ivan has lost his damn mind over a woman, making him forget all about Sidorov and Mariska.

Katya and I spent a few weeks in Omsk while we visited her father and his family, getting familiar with his side and learning more about her roots. There was so much she missed out on, but her relatives were just glad to have her back in their lives even if we had some communication issues.

Unfortunately her Russian isn't coming along so well, but I hope in time she'll be as fluent as the rest of us. Not everyone in the family speaks English like Katya, but they never made her feel bad about it which was wise because I'd lose it if they did. Instead, they'd point to things and say them as we stayed there, so she'd understand a little more. My wife is brilliant, and I know in due time she'll be able to converse with them effortlessly.

That bastard Volchek intentionally kept her from

learning the language just in case she ever caught wind of her mother's death and how it came to be. Everything he did was skilled, and I underestimated his cunning. He may have been a coward, but he was sure one hell of a manipulative son of a bitch.

There was more to Sidorov's story with Katya's mother which is something that I can't even express. If I thought Vlad was terrible, his wife wasn't much better. It's a wonder how Katya came out to be the amazing woman she is.

We've been home for two weeks, and I've been flooded with matter after pressing matter that has kept me busy. Sometimes, missing out on time with my bride which hasn't been good for those around me. I need her to breathe. She restores my sanity with just a smile.

"Knock, knock," Katya says, leaning into my office with her hands pressed on the doorframe. "Lunch is ready."

God, she's stunning. I raise a brow and summon her. "Come over here."

"Nope." She shakes her head, pouting her pretty lips.

"Excuse me?" I tilt my head and stare at the love of my life like she's crazy.

She presses her hands on her hips, giving me a view of the sexy day dress she has on. "I said nope. It's like no, but with more emphasis."

That smart mouth of hers is going to get her into trouble, and I have a feeling she's looking forward to it. "I know what nope means. I'm just wondering why my wife doesn't just come to me when I tell her."

She taps her bare foot on the floor, and I'm instantly aroused by my little garden fairy's painted toes. "Because

I'm not one of your dogs. Besides, I know our lunch will get cold once you get your hands on me."

"Fair point. You are not one of the dogs, but I still am the head of this family. So come over here, woman." She shakes her head again and I'm about to drag her over to spank her pretty little ass.

"My dear wife, it seems someone needs a spanking today," I say, undoing the cuffs and rolling up my sleeves one at a time. She stares and bites down on her bottom lip with anticipation.

I get up from my desk and walk around, stalking toward her. She smiles brightly and blushes because she knows that the second I get my hands on her, we're going to miss lunch completely.

With a quick motion, I flip her over my shoulder, drag her back into my office, and lock the door. I take a seat on the sofa in the corner and set my wife between my legs, belly resting between my open thighs.

She's only two months pregnant and not showing yet, so I've got a little longer for the punishments she loves. Goodness, she does love them. I feel like she tries to push my buttons once or twice a week, so I'll redden her ass and fuck that tight, slick cunt.

Flipping up her dress, I see she's not wearing any fucking panties. "What the hell, Katya? You are really asking for it today."

"I just saved you the trouble." She opens her hand, and there they are, waving a pair of pink and white striped panties.

I take them and bring them to my nose, breathing in her scent before her punishment begins. "Good girl. The idea of anyone getting a peek under your dress, even by accident, would send me into a jealous rage."

"I don't want you to hurt your exemplary employees. This pussy is only for your eyes."

"My hands," I growl, smacking her ass once.

"My cock," I say through clenched teeth.

"Your tongue," she answers as I slap her pussy from behind. Fuck, she's so damn keyed up for a quick fucking.

"Are you horny?" I ask, plunging two fingers into her soaking wet slit.

"Yes. I need you, Roman," she cries out, grabbing onto the cushion as I finger her hole. Sliding out from under her, I set her knees on the sofa while I free my cock from my trousers.

"Stay bent over like that. I'm going to fuck this greedy cunt and if you keep it up, I'm going to have to take this one too." I rub her back entrance, causing her to buck.

Moving into position behind her, I run my tip up and down her seam. "I'll be a good girl."

"You little liar." I push my way into her tight pussy, exhaling as I bottom out inside her. "Hold on, tight, princess." I drill into her sheath over and over with my hands, palming her hips and gliding over her ass, giving it a random spank between thrusts.

"Roman," she shouts. I reach over to cover her mouth and push deeper into her. She groans while I do my best to keep from nutting.

"You keep your voice down, wife. Your cries only belong to me." She nips at my fingers, so I give her what she wants and slide a finger between her lips. "Suck it like it's my cock."

Katya's thighs begin to quake as her orgasm builds and her pussy clenches around my dick. She moans around my finger, and then she sucks hard as her release barrels down on her. Her tight walls flex and choke my length, and I let go, flooding her womb with jet after jet of cum.

I collapse onto her back, using my hands to support most of my weight, but I know she's losing strength. Kissing her spine, I whisper, "I love you, my princess."

"Was I a good girl?" she asks with her head tilted upward, pleased with herself.

"A very good girl, but I'm still debating if you need another punishment."

"We'll see."

"Stay like that," I growl, pulling out to grab some tissues. She turns to her side, resting on the sofa. "See that's what I'm talking about. You don't listen to me at all," I grunt, dropping a kiss down on her lips before I help her get cleaned up.

"I enjoy defying you." She winks and then sucks on one of my fingers.

"Woman, we are really going to miss lunch, and I need to feed you and our little one."

"Well, I might have lied about it being ready," she says as I slide the panties up her legs. As much as I love having my load sliding down her thighs, having her walk around without panties is too much for me to handle.

"Bad girl." She smiles, and I live for that look on her face. Over the past two months, she's come into her own. Being her husband is a blessing and a half.

Her phone buzzes in the pocket of her dress. She pulls it out and says, "Look. Lunch is ready."

It's a text from Maria to let her know the food is done.

I snatched her phone and sent a message back to Maria.

Katya looks down at what I sent and giggles.

Have our lunch brought up to our bedroom. I'm keeping my husband busy for the day with my shenanigans.

After a fabulous lunch, I put on a movie for her, and we relax like a normal couple. She falls asleep halfway through the second movie, but I wake her up just in time for dinner, or so I tell her. It might be a little early for dinner, but I have a taste for dessert, and she never has any complaints.

EPILOGUE

ROMAN

ON MY DESK sits a picture of my parents and Ilya and next to it is a picture of Katya and me at our wedding; they both bring me joy to look at every day as I work. My parents would have adored her and the little life we've created.

It's been six months since my beloved stole my heart when I abducted her and now we're on the verge of having our first child. My chest aches and grows with pride simultaneously. The loss of my parents and the opportunity to meet their grandchildren is something that pangs me every day.

There's a knock on my door that interrupts my thoughts. It has to be my bride because she's the only one to knock so softly. "Come in."

"Roman, can we talk?" I raise my brow at my very pregnant wife, not liking the way she said that.

I stand up and walk around my desk to meet her in the

middle of the room and take her hands in mine. "Of course, my princess. What is it?"

"Well, I know this may seem wrong or maybe it's not something you'd like, but I wanted to know if you considered naming our son after your brother."

I stand there shocked and unmoving, processing her words. "Oh, I knew it was a bad idea." She pulls away from me and starts to cry.

I'm on her in a second, pulling her as close as her belly will allow. Her tears have always been my kryptonite, and I'll do whatever I can to make them stop.

"My heart and soul, I think it's a brilliant and beautiful idea. I'm just stunned that you would want to do that." With all the names she could pick and being that she's used to reading English names, I thought she'd have a favorite to choose from.

I'll never get tired of the way her face lights up with joy. "Really? I love you, Roman and I wish your loved ones could be with us to celebrate this little one and his life."

"I believe we need to celebrate, my little princess." I'm perpetually horny around my wife and I doubt that will stop as we age.

"I'm hardly little anymore." She reminds me, rubbing her large belly, which is so cute on her tiny frame. It's a wonder she can walk at all. My son is going to be massive. Still, it gets another reaction out of me. My dick jerks in my slacks, knowing that I filled her up with my heir.

I turn on the speaker on my phone and let the music play as I twirl my wife around the room. My hand wraps around her waist, holding her as we sway. The longer we stay this close the stiffer my cock gets.

"Katya, I live and breathe for you." We pause mid-song to kiss that slowly turns into a passionate encounter on my desk. Her backside is pressed against the wood, but I need to be closer. I want to hear her come for me. "Lean over and pop that ass out, wife."

She turns around and plants her hands on the surface. Katya whimpers as my hand finds her always-wet pussy. She pushes her mound into my hand to get relief.

"Calm down, my princess. I'm going to make you come so good. You deserve to be rewarded for your thoughtfulness." The music continues to play as I drop behind her and lift her skirt. Sliding her soaked panties off her legs, I tuck them into my pocket.

I drive face first into her sopping heat, eating her pussy while pumping a finger into her tight hole. She thrusts her hips backward, nearly sending me on my ass, but I don't let go of her round ass. I growl and grunt as I munch on her juicy cunt until she coats my face.

When her thighs stop shaking, I slide into her hole with my thick, greedy cock. She's so damn tight, I nearly black out from the pleasure. Holding her by her hips, I pump into her repeatedly while I bite down on her shoulder.

"I love you, Katya. I'll never get enough," I growl as my orgasm slams at the base of my spine. It doesn't take much to send my load shooting into her depths.

"Wow, I have to stop putting on music around you. You get so horny," I tease her as I tuck my cock back into my slacks. Like an animal, I hadn't even bothered to undress either of us.

"Says the man with the constant erection." Yes, and that's probably never going to end unless I get some sort of dysfunction.

I run my hands through my hair and chuckle. "Okay, perhaps more music all the time?" I wag my brows and she slaps my chest.

"Hey, I'm still a little sore there." She gasps, looking to apologize, but I press my hand to her lips. "I'm only teasing."

With a sigh, she lays her head near my heart as we lean against the wooden desk. "Do you have a lot of work to do?"

"No, I'm almost done."

"I'm going to take a shower and then take a nap. If you want, you can join me when you're done." She kisses my cheek and walks out of my office.

I've never moved so quickly to get my job done for the day. Hurrying up to the bedroom, I'm too late to catch her naked. It doesn't matter how many times I see her unclothed, if I get another chance, I want to see her naked again.

My sweet wife is nestled under the covers, wrapped in just her robe. I strip down to my boxers and cling onto her and our little family with everything in me. "I love you both. Sleep, my beauties."

EPILOGUE

KATYA

THE SNOW FALLS all around us as we play in the garden. I hear footsteps behind me and duck and turn before the little body falls on me in a fit of giggles. "Mama." My three-year-old son, Ilya, falls into my arms with his father tagging along behind him.

"I'm sorry, my Princess, but he wouldn't take no for an answer. You shouldn't be doing that." He scolds me as I pick the last of the vegetables from the patch. The season has ended, and winter has begun, and I couldn't pass up the opportunity to pluck up the last bit.

"Sorry, I wanted to make my soup tonight." Roman had a small garden built just for me to remind me of my old one that I enjoyed so much. It's funny how the little things make me happy.

"And we don't have an entire kitchen equipped with everything you need?" he asks, helping me to my feet. Goodness, he looks so handsome in a dark suit with his matching winter coat and his dark hair covered in a dusting of snow. I love this man beyond belief and the life he's given me.

"You married a simple girl from the forest, Roman." I step up on my toes and kiss his lips. With a growl, he slams his mouth on mine and wraps his hand around my waist, dragging me tightly to feel his need even in the cold.

It will forever surprise me how aroused he is around me, although I'm no better than him as my child stands at my feet and another grows inside me.

"Mama, me kiss." I lift him into my arms and kiss his cold nose, bringing a bright smile to his rosy cheeks.

"Smart young man." Roman rubs Ilya's hat-covered head and then takes me around the waist, snatching my vegetable basket from me while leading both of us inside. "Did you get everything you needed for your soup?"

"Yes, I did." I smile up at him, pleased with my success.

"Good. Ilya and I have some matters to discuss while you cook. We'll be down for dinner later."

"Matters to discuss?" I raise my brow, wondering what mischief the two are going to get into. Roman has made the most wonderful father any kid could ask for.

He spends a lot of time with him, giving him almost as much time as he gives me. It's a wonder he can still run his empire. Then again, it's easy when everyone knows you're crazy when it comes to your loved ones and will do anything to protect them. Roman also keeps his business dealings out of the areas that other families have their hands in.

After the whole misstep with the Popov family, Roman has given them the grace that has kept a truce between the families.

"Yes, father to son, discussion."

I twist my lips, knowing they're going to play some more. "Does it have to do with toy soldiers?" No matter how clean Roman likes to keep his hands, he can't fight who he is, which means teaching our son to be strong and strategic.

"Soldiers," Ilya blurts out, clapping his hands. It's his favorite thing to play with in the tub. They were building a snowman, so he needs to get nice and warmed up.

"Okay. Keep your strategies to yourself, and I'll keep my recipes to mine." Roman leans in and steals another kiss before taking our son up to our room to give him a bath.

Maria comes into the kitchen with a grin on her face. "So how about some music while we cook?"

"Sounds great." She puts on the Bluetooth speaker system that fills the kitchen and we rock out to the Beatles while making the soup in bulk. This is the life I'd been missing and thought I'd never have.

I rub my belly, looking forward to the next life already growing inside of me. Tonight, I'll tell him we're expecting another little baby.

EPILOGUE

ROMAN

MY SON just rushed out of my office and I run my hand over my face. "Fuck."

I drop my head back in my chair, thinking about the conversation I just had with Ilya. Is the boy trying to give me a heart attack?

At twenty-five he's become a man I'm proud to say I raised, and my father would have been pleased to know. He's dark, dangerous, and a bit fucking insane— my ruthless prince.

"What's wrong?" Katya says, sauntering into my office in a cute pair of leggings and tight top that beg to be torn off right now.

"Your son."

"Oh so he's my son now? What did he do?" She plops down in my lap, running her fingers through my thick black hair that has turned partially gray. I can't imagine why given her little ass gave me a bunch of heathens that are just as crazy as me and then some.

"Drago came to visit with his family in Omsk while Ilya was handling some matters for me," I grumble.

"Oh no. Did he have a problem with Drago's son?" They aren't the best friends which is ridiculous considering Drago's Ilya's godfather.

"No. His daughter."

"What happened with Natalya?" she gasps.

"Right now, I'm assuming she's tied to his bed, and I'm waiting for my friend to come barreling down my door and wanting my son's head." She opens her eyes wide and covers her mouth, but I'm not buying it. My little bride has secrets in her pretty eyes. That was the fakest look of shock I've ever seen. I'm about to bend her ass over and spank her.

My phone rings and Katya answers it, putting it on speaker, "Hello, Drago. How are you?" Her voice is saccharinely sweet, knowing that he's furious on the other end.

"Where is he?" he barks out. I'd be pissed about his attitude, but I'd kill someone who took my princess. Still, if he was in front of me, I'd hard pressed not to punch him in his balls.

"Who? Roman?" my devilish wife asks while smirking at me and running her hands through my hair. I have to fight a groan and a growing arousal. I slap her ass.

"Ilya. The little shit." There's nothing little about my boy except his patience.

"Come on now. He's like six-five, that would make him a big shit," she says with a playful pout as if Drago could see her face. Possessively, I'm grateful he can't because she's still as sexy as ever.

"I don't give a shit either way. Ilya either better return

my baby girl back to me pristine or there better be a ring on her finger," he snarls.

"Of course, he will marry her," Rosalyn says over the line, probably trying to calm him down. "Have you missed the crazy in his eyes? You men scream insane when it comes to us women."

"It's true. You men are nuts."

"I don't care. She's my baby."

"Katya, ignore Drago. It's all his fault. He shouldn't have tried to introduce her to Anatoly's son who has grown up to be a handsome man."

"Hey, woman," Drago snarls at his wife.

"I'm just saying you dangled another man in front of a boy who has been obsessed with our princess. What did you expect? Would you like it if I was there flirting with another man?"

"Don't even dare." I can picture Drago snapping a fucker's neck for even daring to speak to his wife. I'd do the same if someone was foolish enough to speak to my wife.

"We'll get the wedding plans underway," Katya says, grabbing her planner off my desk and looking through it happily. "I'll make some calls today."

"Good." Drago sounds distracted, so Katya ends the call.

Smiling at me with a look of pure triumph. "See. Easy as pie. Now, does he really have her tied to the bed?"

I shrug my shoulders. "Probably, he did kidnap her."

She rolls her eyes. "Shit. This is going to be fun. In the meantime…" She rakes her hand over my shirt. "… I think you should thank me for handling that so well."

"Oh, yes?"

"Yes." She nods and then scoots up on the desk and

parts her thighs with an open invitation to her slick pussy that I could almost make out through those tight leggings.

With a yank on the material, I tear open them right at the seam. Her pussy is instantly revealed to me. I'm wondering if she didn't already get a call from Rosalyn before I spoke to my son.

"I suppose you were a very good girl." I have to reward her and myself. "Or have you? How long have you been handling it?"

"Um…Rosalyn might have mentioned a visit months ago."

"Bad girl. You need to see how crazy us men are," I growl.

"Good or bad…does it make a difference?"

"No. It truly doesn't, my wife." I dip my tongue into her hole and feast until she's coming on my face. Then I take my fill with her face pressed onto the wooden surface of my desk and my cock buried balls deep into her womb.

I have her pinned to the desk when the phone rings again. "We're busy. It better be important."

"Damn, tell him to hurry up, girl. We have to talk about wedding plans," Rosalyn says, giggling on the other end.

"Sorry, girl. Give me five minutes." I fix my clothes and shake my head at these too. They are too sneaky for our own good. Drago and I need to start being a little concerned.

"Don't worry. Angry fucks are so much faster…but a lot of fun. Call me back," she says, hanging up with a giggle.

"Don't worry, we have daughters someone will try to steal from us one day too."

"No they won't," I snarl.

"Okay…"

"You better text, Rosalyn that you're going to need some time," I growl, snatching the blanket off the back of my sofa in my office and carrying her right out of the room.

She giggles. "Okay."

THE END

ABOUT THE AUTHOR

FIND MORE ABOUT CARINA BLAKE
   www.carinablake.com
   www.facebook.com/AuthorCarinaBlake/
   www.amazon.com/Carina-Blake/e/B088SGRYWL
   www.bookbub.com/profile/carina-blake

OTHER BOOKS BY CARINA BLAKE:
STOLEN HEARTS SERIES:

Stolen Wife

Stolen Dove

Stolen Tutor

Dark Reign:

Ruthless Kingpin

Bratva Prince

Printed in Great Britain
by Amazon